The Old Bakehouse

Daphne Neville

Copyright © 2019 Daphne Neville

All rights reserved, including the right to reproduce this book, or portions thereof in any form. No part of this text may be reproduced, transmitted, downloaded, decompiled, reverse engineered, or stored, in any form or introduced into any information storage and retrieval system, in any form or by any means, whether electronic or mechanical without the express written permission of the author.

This is a work of fiction. Names and characters are the product of the author's imagination and any resemblance to actual persons, living or dead, is entirely coincidental.

The views expressed in this work are solely those of the author and do not necessarily reflect the views of the publisher, and the publisher hereby disclaims any responsibility for them.

ISBN: 978-0-244-47174-3

PublishNation
www.publishnation.co.uk

Other Titles by This Author

TRENGILLION CORNISH MYSTERY SERIES
The Ringing Bells Inn
Polquillick
Sea, Sun, Cads and Scallywags
Grave Allegations
The Old Vicarage
A Celestial Affair
Trengillion's Jubilee Jamboree

PENTRILLICK CORNISH MYSTERY SERIES
The Chocolate Box Holiday
A Pasty In A Pear Tree
The Suitcase in the Attic
Tea and Broken Biscuits

The Old Tile House

Chapter One

One morning in early September, Kitty Thomas crossed the road outside the Crown and Anchor public house and stepped into Long Lane where she hurriedly walked up the hill carrying a basket of shopping. Although in her late sixties Kitty was fit for her age; she walked a lot, talked a lot and kept her weight down. Nevertheless, she was convinced that Long Lane was steeper than when she was younger; longer too for that matter. When she reached the top of the hill, she turned right into Blackberry Way where to her delight she saw sexagenarian twin sisters, Hetty and Lottie, pulling weeds from a flower bed in the front garden of their home, Primrose Cottage.

"I've just come up from the village," puffed Kitty, as she leaned on the front garden wall. "There's quite a buzz in the post office this morning because word's just got out that old Joe Williams is dead."

Hetty dropped a handful of dandelion seedlings into a bucket and then stood up to ease her back. "Who on earth is old Joe Williams? I'm sure I've not heard that name mentioned before."

Kitty frowned. "Hmm, no, on reflection I suppose you wouldn't have. He used to be the baker here many moons ago as did his father, grandfather and great grandfather before him. In fact, it probably goes back even further than that because the Old Bakehouse is one of the oldest buildings in the village and it's always been a bakehouse. Well, it was, it's not now and hasn't been since I was a nipper and that's going back a bit."

"So, whereabouts is it?" Hetty removed her gardening gloves and dropped them into her bucket of weeds.

"On the corner just before the Pentrillick Hotel and next door to the hairdressers."

"Oh, you know where it is, Het," said Lottie, "it's the shabby looking place with mullioned windows."

Kitty nodded. "Yes, that's the one."

Lottie stood up and brushed loose soil from her kneeler. "Come on, let's go indoors for a coffee and then you can tell us more. That's unless you're in a hurry to get home."

Kitty turned and took a few steps back towards the open gates. "No, I've all the time in the world. Tommy's out this morning so I don't even have to bother with lunch."

Kitty and her husband Tommy, both retired, were near neighbours of Hetty and Lottie and lived at Meadowsweet, the last of eight houses that made up Blackberry Way; an idyllic spot which overlooked the seaside village of Pentrillick.

"So why is the death of this old baker causing a buzz?" Lottie asked, as they sat around the living room table with mugs of coffee and a plate of biscuits.

Kitty laughed. "Well, I'm not really sure but it's probably because it seemed he'd live forever. Most reckoned he'd make a hundred and they were even planning to see that he got a birthday card from the Queen. He was certainly the oldest person in the village."

Hetty was intrigued. "So how old was he?"

"Ninety-nine so I'm told and he'd have been a hundred next January."

Hetty sighed. "Oh dear, he nearly made it then."

"A good age nevertheless," acknowledged Lottie, "especially if he was still living at home."

"It certainly is," agreed Kitty, "and yes he was still living at home and it's said he was able to look after himself right up until the end. Apparently he died in his sleep and was found by Karen and Nicki when they opened up the hairdressers this morning. You see, they were concerned because Joe's little dog was barking and seemed distressed and so they popped round to see if he was alright. Joe didn't answer the door when they knocked and so they went in. As they called out his name, Crumpet, he's the dog, came running down the stairs and seemed to want them to follow him. They did and found Joe dead in his bed."

"Nice way to go," said Lottie.

Hetty tutted. "Hmm, not so nice for Karen and Nicki though."

"No," agreed Kitty, "it's said they're quite upset. They often used to pop in to make sure he was okay, you see and Karen used to take the dog for a walk during her lunch break."

"So out of curiosity, did he have any family?" Lottie asked.

"Ah, now that's the sixty-four-million-dollar question," chuckled Kitty, "He did but as far as I know he's not seen anything of his offspring for years. His first wife died in childbirth donkey's years ago and I believe the child was adopted. Sometime later he married again and he and his new wife had a son but then suddenly she, the new wife, got up and left him and took the boy with her. Rumour has it she had another chap but whatever the reason old Joe was never the same again. He closed up the bakery after she went despite the fact it was a highly profitable business and he never baked another loaf again."

Hetty tutted. "Poor chap. How long ago was that?"

"About sixty years I'd say. As I said earlier, I was only a nipper and I wouldn't have remembered at all were it not for the chat in the post office this morning."

"Poor, poor man," said Lottie, "how horrible to have lost two wives and two children."

Kitty looked over the top of her glasses. "Well, yes, I suppose so but it's said he was a real ladies man in his day and a shocking flirt so that's probably what drove the second wife away."

Hetty laughed as she dunked a chocolate biscuit in her coffee and quickly took a bite before the chocolate melted. "And it's probably why the bakery was a profitable business."

"So what'll happen to the Old Bakehouse now? Will it be sold do you think?" Lottie asked.

Kitty shrugged her shoulders. "I suppose so. Time will tell no doubt but from what was said this morning I reckon it's pretty rundown."

Hetty looked at her sister. "Are you thinking about Bill and Sandra?"

Lottie nodded. "Well yes, a rundown property in the heart of the village sounds the perfect place for the family to live in, providing the price is right of course."

"And that it's big enough," Hetty added.

"Are your family thinking of moving down here then?" Kitty was surprised.

"Yes, they've been talking about it for some time and if you remember we told you back in June that Sandra's widowed mother had died. Bill rang yesterday to say they've just finalised the sale of her house and so because Sandra was an only child, they now have a substantial sum of money and they want to put it towards a property down here. Then of course they'd have the money from the sale of their own place which even after the mortgage is paid off will be a tidy sum."

"And as luck would have it," added Hetty, "Bill and Sandra's next door neighbour has let it be known that if they ever want to sell up and move to Cornwall then he'd like the chance to buy it. The houses are semi-detached, you see, and he'd like to knock the two into one."

"Ideal," said Kitty, "but what would your Bill do about work?"

"He works for one of the large supermarket chains and so can get a transfer down here. He's already asked and so it shouldn't be a problem."

Kitty frowned. "And the children? What about their schooling?"

Lottie sighed. "Hmm, that's not so good I must admit. Zac will be okay because he's finished his A-levels and is now looking for a job. The girls, however, have just started theirs and so it will mean finding them another school."

"Ah, but they're bright girls so they'd soon adapt I'm sure," Kitty acknowledged.

"Yes, they will," agreed Hetty, "and the entire family is so keen to move down here that I'm sure we'll be able to sort everything out."

"And if the Old Bakehouse does come up for sale and is a suitable proposition the family could stay here for a while if any major work needed to be done," added Lottie.

"Sounds perfect then," enthused Kitty, "I'll give Tess a ring when I get home and put her in the picture. She's sure to know what's going on before anyone else."

The following morning, Kitty called again. "Tess just rang. She's been asking around and says she's finally found out that the Old Bakehouse is to be sold and the estate agents are hoping to have details on their website by Saturday lunchtime. She doesn't know which agents are dealing with the sale though but the solicitors handling the will are the ones young Kyle works for but she couldn't remember what they're called. I've been wracking my brains too but I've drawn a blank, however Tommy reckons there's a Tremayne somewhere in the name. Not that that's a great deal of help."

"Hmm, well I haven't the foggiest idea," sighed Hetty, "I don't think I've ever even heard the name mentioned."

Lottie agitatedly twisted the wedding ring on her finger. "Well we must try and find out because I should imagine there will be quite a bit of interest in the place when it first gets advertised. I rang Bill last night, Kitty, to tell him about it and he sounded quite excited at the prospect of living in an old bakehouse."

"That's good to hear, and yes, you're right. Houses in the village always get snapped up pretty quickly so there's no time to waste."

"So how can we find out more? We need the name of the estate agents or the solicitors," Lottie felt panic stricken.

"I suppose you could ask your grandson to find out," suggested Kitty, "After all he and Kyle seemed to get on well together."

Hetty slapped her knees. "Of course, it's the obvious solution. You must ring Zac, Lottie."

"But will Kyle be allowed to pass on information like that? I mean surely it'd be unethical to pass on personal details and I don't want to get him into trouble."

Hetty shook her head. "No, we only want to know the name of the estate agents who'll be handling the sale so that we can keep an eye on their website. I can't see as that will be a problem."

"You're right," Lottie stood up, "I'll ring Zac right now."

Inside the offices of Tremayne, Watts and Braithwaite, Solicitors, Kyle said goodbye to his work colleagues and stepped outside into the late afternoon sunshine. From his pocket he pulled a bunch of keys and jangled them as he walked to the small staff car park where his new car gleamed in the sunlight. With pride he unlocked the door, stepped inside and began the short drive home to Pentrillick.

Kyle was very happy with life; he had done well in his university studies and had received a worthy degree in law for his efforts. He was now in his third week of working as a trainee solicitor and he loved every minute of it.

As he pulled up on the pavement outside the house where he lived with his parents, his mobile phone rang. To his surprise it was Zac, a friend he had first made when the Burton family were on holiday in Pentrillick back in the summer of 2016.

"Hiya, mate. Is everything okay?"

"Yes, everything's fine but I've a favour to ask."

"Okay, what is it?"

"Is your office handling the will and estate of some chap in the village called Joe who was a baker? Apparently, he died yesterday."

"Oh, you mean Joe Williams. Yes, we are. Why do you ask?"

"Because if the place where this old Joe lived is to be sold, Grandma thinks it might be of interest to us lot. Mum and Dad are dead keen so we desperately need to know the name of the estate agents so that we can get in quick. If it's to be sold, that is."

"You mean there's a chance you might be moving down here?" The smile on Kyle's face spread.

"Yep, looks that way."

"Wow, that's brill news, Zac. I hope you do then you can join the pool team."

Zac laughed. "That's just what I thought."

"Anyway, I know it's definitely going to be sold but I can't tell you the name of the estate agents right now simply because I don't who they are but I'll find out tomorrow and message you straight away."

"Cheers, Kyle. I appreciate that."

Chapter Two

Just before midday on the following Monday morning, Lottie's son Bill, and Sandra, his wife left their Northamptonshire home for the drive to Cornwall and, because they intended to be away for no more than two days, they left their three children, Zac aged eighteen and the sixteen-year-old twins, Kate and Vicki to fend for themselves. At first the twins had objected but then agreed it was silly to miss school, especially if the Old Bakehouse proved to be an unsuitable future home.

After they had crossed the Tamar Bridge, Bill and Sandra drove through Cornwall and eventually joined the A394. Several miles later after they had passed through Helston they turned into the lane which led down to Pentrillick. The sun was setting over the rooftops as they drove along the main street and up towards Primrose Cottage where they were to stay with Hetty and Lottie.

The following morning, Bill and Sandra were up bright and early and after breakfast walked down into the village where they were due to meet someone from Thomas Bolitho Estate Agents' office. They purposely arrived early for the appointment so they were able to take a good look at the property from the outside.

"Looks like there's no parking," Bill glanced around the corner of the house into Goose Lane where a solid green door led into the back garden, "so we'd have to park on the street."

"Well it did say that in the details on the agents' website and it's probably a good thing because it might put other potential buyers off." Sandra attempted to peer in through one of the downstairs windows but her vision was blocked by net curtains.

"Did it? I must have missed that bit." Bill noted the paint on the front door was peeling badly. "Having the entrance of the house opening out onto the pavement should put people off too. I'm not sure whether I like it or not."

Sandra laughed. "Well it was a shop so I suppose it's to be expected. I just hope there aren't lots of things to put *us* off because at the moment we've only found fault. I don't think I mind it opening out onto the street but I do object to that door, it's hideous."

"It is, and that'll be the first thing to go."

"Oh, no it won't because if you remember the building is Grade Two listed so the door will have to stay."

"But it's not the original," groaned Bill, "it looks like something from the fifties or sixties."

"It doesn't matter. If that's the door that was here when it was listed then that's the door that will have to stay."

"Oh dear, well never mind. Let's be positive: after all the house is in a nice location in a village we love and I reckon from the upstairs windows on the front you'd be able to see the sea over the rooftops of the houses opposite, so that's three positive things."

"And it's right next door to the hairdressers," laughed Sandra, "so there will be no excuse for me ever having messy hair. I also like the fact it's on a corner."

As she spoke a car pulled up by the pavement and a young man wearing a dark suit stepped out. He offered his hand. "Mr and Mrs Burton, I assume."

"Correct," Bill shook the proffered hand and Sandra did likewise.

The front door of the Old Bakehouse led straight into a good sized area which would in the past have been the shop but which since its closure Joe had used as a dining area. From it a door led into a spacious hallway where a straight, steep staircase ran to the upper floor; a door opposite led into a large sitting room with an inglenook fireplace; two windows on the front looked into the street and French doors at the back led into the garden. Upstairs there were four bedrooms, and a bathroom with an ancient suite and overhead toilet cistern; the water appeared to be heated from a boiler hanging precariously on the wall above the bath and the lino covering the floor was worn and brittle.

Back downstairs they returned to the original shop area where a door in the back wall led into a small kitchenette; beyond it was a large square room with a flagstone floor where the bread would have been baked. It was obvious from the state of the room that it had not been used for many years. Two huge industrial electric ovens stood on one side of the room opposite freestanding cupboards; an old Belfast sink sat beneath a deep sill and a dirty window covered in cobwebs. Near to the sink a half-glazed door led into a large porch which looked to be a recent addition to the house. The porch led into the back garden which to Sandra's delight appeared much bigger than she had anticipated from pictures shown on the agents' website. It was surrounded by high stone walls and overgrown with weeds and brambles; a granite bird bath sat beneath an apple tree and a broken bird table stood amongst tall seed heads of grass in an area which had once been a lawn. There was also a large outhouse with an old wooden work bench and tools hanging from the walls draped in cobwebs and peppered with dust.

"So, what do you think?" Bill asked his wife as they sat in Taffeta's Tea Shoppe to mull over their thoughts.

"I liked it. It's roomy and airy and I think it has great potential. With four bedrooms the children would be able to have one each and I'm itching to get out in that garden to knock it back into shape."

Bill smiled. "I knew that would appeal and I agree with you about the house. A new bathroom would have to take priority and of course getting central heating fitted, and even if we had to pay the asking price we'd still have enough money to pay for the renovation work including having a wood burner fitted in the big sitting room because I know you'll want that."

"Good heavens, yes, and it would look fantastic in that large inglenook fireplace."

"What about the kitchenette? Could we manage with that until we got the old baking room converted into a kitchen?"

Sandra nodded. "Of course making do would be all part of the fun."

"And what about the children? Do you think they'll like it?"

"Without doubt. All three of them are so eager to move down here I think they'd even be happy living in a wooden shack."

Bill drained his coffee mug and placed it back on its saucer. "We better put an offer in then because we know there is a lot of interest in the old place and as there's no time like the present, I'll do it now."

Lottie was delighted to hear that Bill and Sandra liked the Old Bakehouse and had already put in an offer before they returned to Primrose Cottage for lunch. She was happier still when Bill received a phone call later that afternoon to say the offer had been accepted.

"I can't wipe the smile off my face," she said the next morning after Bill and Sandra had left for the drive home, "It's just too good to be true. Little did I realise when we all came on holiday in 2016 that we'd *all* end up living here."

"Well don't count the chickens before they're hatched," advised Hetty, dreading that her sister might yet be disappointed, "as all sorts can go wrong when it comes to buying and selling houses. Although I suppose with the Old Bakehouse being empty and Bill and Sandra's buyer being pretty solid there's no reason why it should fall through."

Lottie stood up. "Let's go down to the charity shop and see if we can find out a bit more about Joe the baker then I can pass it on to Bill and Sandra."

"Good idea, but we must be subtle as we don't want to look too nosy."

"So, what can you tell us about the wives of the late Joe Williams?" Hetty casually asked Maisie and Daisy as they arrived at the village charity shop on pretence of looking at the books.

"Not a great deal," admitted Daisy, "because I don't remember either. Joe's first wife died in childbirth and that was before I was born, poor soul. The second did a runner when I was very young. Sadly, I don't know any more than that."

Maisie nodded. "Same goes for me. I wish I knew more as it's the talk of the village at present but it's no good trying to wrack my brains because I know there's no memory there to recall."

As if on cue, Tess Dobson, a lady who worked part-time in the bar of the Crown and Anchor and who was well acquainted with village gossip, entered the shop.

"Ah, here's someone who might know something," teased Daisy as the latest arrival closed the shop door. "We're talking about Joe Williams and his wives, Tess. What have you learned?"

Tess smirked. "Funny you should ask that because I've just bumped into Lucy Lacey and it occurred to me that her being in her seventies, she might remember the wives and what it was like here when the bakery was a going concern."

Daisy produced a chair from behind the counter. "Sit down, Tess. We're all ears."

"Thank you. Well Lucy doesn't remember the first wife, the one who died in childbirth but she knows the child was adopted when a few weeks old because Joe wouldn't have been able to have coped with a baby and run the bakery business as well."

Maisie nodded. "Certainly, would have been very difficult."

"Was the baby a girl or a boy, do you know?" Hetty asked.

Tess shook her head. "Lucy wasn't sure."

"I wonder why the wife's parents didn't look after the child," puzzled Lottie, "or Joe's parents for that matter."

"That's exactly what I said to Lucy and her response was she recalls her mum mentioning that Joe's mother was in poor health so it would have been too much for her and as for the parents of Joe's late wife, it appears they disapproved of the marriage and so wanted nothing to do with the child anyway."

"That seems rather harsh," cried Lottie, "poor little mite. I hope he or she went to a good home."

"That's just what I said," Tess acknowledged, "but sadly Lucy has no idea where the child went. It might not even have been somewhere in Cornwall."

"Was the first wife a local girl?" Hetty wondered, "I ask thinking there could be some of her relatives still around."

Tess shook her head. "No, apparently Joe met her during the war and they were married up country somewhere or other then after the war they returned to Pentrillick."

"So who baked the bread during the war?"

"Joe's parents, I assume. I get the impression it was after the war that Joe took over the business. His parents lost a son in 1941. Killed in action as they say and it badly affected his mother's health."

"So Joe lost a brother." Lottie tutted: "how sad."

"Was he married?" Hetty asked. "The brother, that is."

"No, he was younger than Joe and only in his teens. Lucy recalls her parents talking about him with affection and for that reason it always brought a lump her throat when she heard his name read out amongst others in church on Remembrance Sundays."

Daisy sat down on a pile of books which needed sorting. "Okay, we get the gist, Tess, so please continue."

"Well, there's not really much more to say but Lucy reckons it was when she was about ten years old that Joe married again. His new wife was called Eve and they had a son called Norman. Lucy said Eve worked in the baker's shop and was ever so nice. She often went in there you see because Joe made fantastic pasties."

"So Joe did pastry as well as bread." Hetty was surprised.

"Oh yes, he was the proper job."

"It must have taken him forever to produce enough to feed a village this size," reasoned Lottie.

"Well, I suppose not everyone shopped in the village and I think the Co-op used to deliver bread as well, I remember my mum telling me they did that when she was a girl. Then on top of that the village was smaller back then as lots of places weren't built 'til after the war."

"Of course. Anyway, what happened next?"

Tess shrugged her shoulders. "Lucy said nobody quite knows for sure but it's said that one day Eve suddenly packed her bags and left. It's rumoured she left a note for Joe saying she'd met someone else which ties in with what's being said on the grapevine today but I don't know whether that's true or not. Anyway, after she left Joe closed the bakery and it's been closed ever since."

Hetty tutted.

"So what did he do after that?" Lottie asked, "I mean, he would only have been a young man surely so he'd have needed to work to live and pay the bills."

"That's right he did and he went to work as one of the groundsmen at Pentrillick House and Lucy's father would have known him because he was working there too. In fact that's probably why Lucy knows a bit more than most as I daresay her parents talked about Joe and his circumstances."

"Hmm, so if Joe and Eve's son was born when Lucy was around ten years of age then there's every chance that he's still living," mused Lottie, "I wonder where."

"What did you say his name was, Tess?" Hetty asked.

"Norman, Norman Williams and Lucy reckons he'd be in his early sixties now."

Chapter Three

Norman Williams sat on the sitting room floor of the Dawlish home he had shared with his parents for as long as he could remember. In his hand he held the death certificate of his recently deceased mother and was searching for the death certificate of his late father so that both could be stored together. He found the certificate sought in a large brown envelope along with condolence cards and the invoice and receipt from the undertaker who had conducted his father's funeral.

Realising his mother had seldom spoken of the past he looked to see if he could find his parents' marriage certificate for he was ashamed to admit that he'd no idea where they had married and when. He found an envelope marked birth certificates and another containing the deeds of the house together with his mother's driving licence but there appeared to be no sign of a marriage certificate. As he puzzled as to where it might be there was a knock on the back door and the familiar voice of his next door neighbour, Jackie, who had helped to nurse his mother during the last months of her life.

"Only me, Norman," Jackie called, her head poked around the door.

"Come in, come in," he shouted so that Jackie would hear, "I'm in the front room."

She entered and found him sitting on the floor surrounded by the contents of the empty drawer by his side. "Having a clear out?"

"Hmm, yes and no. At the moment I'm actually looking for my parents' marriage certificate but for some reason I can't find it."

Jackie sat down on the floor with legs crossed and surveyed the mass of papers, envelopes and old photographs. "Perhaps they never got married then. Have you ever seen pictures of their wedding?" She glanced up at the walls where a few photographs hung above an overloaded bookcase.

Norman frowned. "No, now you come to mention it I haven't. How strange."

"Yeah, it is because people from your parents' generation usually have pictures of their weddings on pianos, sideboards or whatever so it looks to me like they never tied the knot."

"But they must have been married. I mean back in the fifties it'd have been frowned on if they weren't, especially after I was born."

Jackie giggled. "Yes, living in sin I think they called it."

"Ah, but they were definitely married because Mum always called herself Mrs Williams." Norman picked up several envelopes and returned them to the drawer.

"Well I suppose she called herself Mrs Williams so that everyone would think they were married. I mean no-one would have reason to doubt it, would they?"

Norman shook his head, then he smiled. "No, but I can prove they married because the name on Mum's driving licence is Evelyn Florence Williams and you can't fake that." Norman pulled the licence from the brown envelope and showed it to Jackie.

"Hmm, but then perhaps Williams was your mother's maiden name, if so it wouldn't have changed, would it? After all it's quite a common name." Jackie was confident she was right.

Norman shook his head. "No, I don't think it was Williams, in fact I'm sure it wasn't." He reached for the envelope marked birth certificates and looked inside.

"Johns," he chortled, triumphantly, "of course, that's right, I remember now her maiden name was Evelyn Florence Johns and she was born in Cornwall." He passed the birth certificate for Jackie to look at.

"Alright, I'm convinced, and if you still can't find the marriage certificate but want to know the details you could always check it out online anyway."

"Can I? How?"

"By going on one of the ancestry search websites. I'm a member of one because I'm doing our family tree for Mum and Dad so the search won't cost you anything if I do it. Shall we have a look?" Jackie scrambled to her feet.

"Yes, I think we should because I'd like to get to the bottom of this."

Norman fetched his laptop from the kitchen and Jackie logged into her account. "Right, so what are your parents' full names and when might they have got married?"

Norman shrugged his shoulders. "Mum was Evelyn Florence Johns and Dad was Oscar Patterson Williams and I was born in 1956 so I suppose they were married a year or so before that."

Jackie typed in the names for 1955. Evelyn Florence Johns came up but the only Williams on the page was a Joseph Percival Williams.

Norman scratched his head. "That doesn't make sense. Dad was definitely Oscar Patterson Williams. Patterson was his mother's maiden name."

"Do you have his birth certificate?"

"Yes, of course," Norman took the certificate from the envelope and handed it to Jackie. She scratched her head. "Hmm, you're right. How strange."

"Try the year earlier."

Jackie typed in the names of Norman's parents for 1954 but there were no matches for either.

"Shall I order a copy of the marriage certificate for Evelyn Florence Johns and Joseph Percival Williams?"

"Can you do that?"

"Of course. It'd have to be paid for but will be worth it to clear the mystery up. I've ordered several certificates for my family in recent years and they're quite fascinating."

"Well we could do but it'd be a waste of money if it turns out they're not the right people. I mean Dad's name was Oscar there's no doubt about that."

"Do you have *your* birth certificate?" Jackie asked.

Norman's face brightened. "Yes, of course. That'll confirm Dad's name, won't it?"

When he took the certificate from the envelope and read the name Joseph Percival Williams, his face dropped. "I...I... don't understand."

Jackie looked over his shoulder." And you were born in Cornwall the same as your mum."

"Yes, so I was. I didn't even know that."

"Have you never read your birth certificate before now?" Jackie looked confused.

"No, not really. The only time I recall needing it was when I applied for a provisional driving licence but that was years ago and I daresay Mum dealt with most of the paperwork. She usually did because she knew I hated filling in forms and stuff like that."

"Hmm, or did she volunteer to do it so that you had no reason to see the certificate yourself?"

Four days later when Jackie arrived home from work her mother said there was a letter for her; she instantly recognised the envelope propped up on the kitchen table between the pepper and salt. Knowing it would be the marriage certificate she ate her dinner with gusto, said goodbye to her parents and then hurried next door to see Norman. His fingers shook as he attempted to open the envelope and twice it slipped from his hands.

"Give it me, butterfingers," said Jackie understanding his anxiety.

She opened the envelope and handed its contents to Norman without looking at it. He gasped. The certificate confirmed details of the marriage between Evelyn Florence Johns aged twenty and Joseph Percival Williams aged thirty-six. The wedding took place on June 11th 1955 at St. Mary's Church, Pentrillick, Cornwall. Evelyn's occupation was machinist; Joseph was a baker.

"So…so, the man Oscar who I've believed to be my father all these years, wasn't my father at all." Norman sat down, the colour had drained from his face.

"It certainly looks that way."

"I suppose that's why I could never see any similarity between me and the man I thought was my dad. I mean, he was always nicely dressed and didn't like getting his hands dirty where as I'm the outdoor type when I'm not at work, that is. He was also on the short size and thin where as I'm…," Norman looked down at his pudgy waist, "well, I suppose I'm a bit porky."

"But you're tall so you can carry it off," said Jackie kindly.

Norman smiled. "Fancy a trip to Cornwall? I'd like to find out a bit more about this Joseph Percival Williams."

"You'd like me to go with you?" Jackie was surprised and flattered.

"Yes, because you're into this family history thing."

"Then the answer's definitely yes because I've never been to Cornwall."

"You don't think your parents will mind, do you?"

"Norman, I'm not a baby."

"No, of course not. I'll tell them what it's all about anyway. I'm sure they'll understand."

"No need because I already have," said Jackie, "and they're as intrigued as you and me."

"Really! So when shall we go?"

"Well, if you're game we can go this weekend because I've got the weekend off for a change. We can set off after you finish work on Friday and then leave to come back on Sunday afternoon."

"Okay, but we'll need somewhere to stay and I'll need someone to feed Muffins."

"I'll get Mum to pop in and feed the cat after all she's only next door so it won't be any bother."

Jackie picked up her mobile phone and looked for accommodation. "Brilliant. There's a hotel in the village and it has vacancies. Shall I book us a twin room? It'd be cheaper than two singles."

"That's fine with me if you don't mind sharing."

"Of course I don't mind sharing." She laughed. "It might raise a few eyebrows. On the other hand the people who run the hotel will probably think you're my dad."

Norman chuckled. "Granddad more like."

The chance of anyone thinking the two were related was very slim. Norman had blue eyes, he was tall, overweight, clean shaven and white haired. Jackie on the other hand was petite. She had short spikey jet black hair, multiple ear piercings and tattoos on her fingers. Her eyes were brown and she looked younger than her twenty-two years.

Norman and Jackie arrived in Pentrillick just after eight o'clock on Friday evening and after they had booked into the hotel they took a walk through the village hopeful of finding the Crown and Anchor, a pub of which Jackie had read details on her phone. On the way they passed the Old Bakehouse and noticed that the estate agent's board outside indicated the property was for sale and under offer.

"Hey, this is probably where your dad did his baking many years ago," said Jackie, pausing to peer in through a downstairs window, "it looks pretty rundown and creepy."

Norman stepped out onto the road to get a better view of the property. "You could well be right and if you are, I wonder how long ago it stopped being a bakery."

"Be interesting to find out."

Norman stepped back onto the pavement. "Can you see anything through there?"

"Not really. There's a net curtain in the way and the only bit I can see through is at the end where it doesn't quite meet the wall." Jackie moved to another window but again her view was obstructed by another net curtain.

"Well, hopefully someone in the pub will be able to tell us a bit about the old place."

They resumed their walk.

"Providing we can find the pub," giggled Jackie, "there's no sign of it yet."

"Be patient," laughed Norman, "we've only come a few yards."

They eventually found the Crown and Anchor at the far end of the village on the left hand side of the road opposite a narrow lane.

"Cool," shrieked Jackie, as she opened the pub door, "you must be able to see the beach out the back. A pint of lager while watching the sea sounds right up my street."

"In the summer maybe but not on a chilly evening in September."

Inside the pub, Tess Dobson was working in the bar alongside licensees Ashley and Alison Rowe. Norman asked Tess for two pints of lager.

"I wonder, umm, do you know anything about the Old Bakehouse?" he inquired, as Tess placed the full glasses on the bar, "I see it's for sale and I'm curious to know how long ago it used to be a bakery."

"It hasn't been a bakery in my lifetime," Tess conceded, "and as far as I know it stopped selling bread back in 1958."

Norman handed Tess a ten pound note. "Two years after I was born then, that is a long time. Any idea what happened to the chap who was the baker back in those days? I have reason to believe his name was Joseph Percival Williams."

"Yes, that's right. We all knew him as Joe but sadly he's no longer with us." Tess handed Norman his change.

"Not surprised about that as I daresay he'd be a ripe old age if he were still alive."

"Well, he did live to a good age. He was ninety-nine and lots of us thought he'd make it to a hundred and we planned to get a birthday card sent to him from the Queen. It's funny you should be asking about him though because he only passed away the other day and his funeral is next Monday."

"Are you alright, Norman?" Jackie asked as Tess moved on to serve the next customer, "You've gone awfully pale." Jackie took Norman's arm and guided him towards a table near to closed French doors which led out onto a sun terrace. She then fetched the two glasses of lager from the bar.

"I can't believe he was still alive until a few days ago." Norman picked up his glass and took several gulps, "If only I'd known about him earlier I could have met him, if he wanted to meet me, that is. Now it's too late. Although if I'm honest I didn't in my wildest dreams expect him still to be alive anyway."

"We must stay for an extra couple of days," Jackie was touched by the tears welling in Norman's eyes, "and we'll go to his funeral. At least there you might learn something about him. Someone might even have a picture and if not there's bound to be one on the order of service thing."

As Tess served the next customer, she suddenly began to wonder why the chap who bought two lagers and who she had never seen before had wanted to know about the Old Bakehouse and Joe in particular. So when Hetty approached the bar Tess told her of the request and nodded over to the table where Norman and Jackie sat.

"Hmm," mused Hetty, instantly intrigued, "leave it with me, Tess and I'll see if I can find out who they are."

After purchasing two glasses of wine, Hetty approached the table in question.

"Sorry to bother you but the lady behind the bar just told me that you were asking about Joe Williams and the Old Bakehouse. I didn't know the gentleman because I've not lived in the village very long but I do know a bit about the bakehouse because my nephew and his wife are in the throes of buying it."

Norman's face lit up. "I'd love to hear anything you can tell me. Anything at all."

"Then come and sit with us. We're over by the fire."

As they reached the table and took their seats, Hetty rested her hand on Lottie's shoulder.

"I'm Hetty by the way and this is my twin sister, Lottie."

"I'm Norman and this young lady is my next door neighbour and good friend, Jackie."

Hetty frowned. "Norman, not Norman Williams by any chance?"

"Well, actually, yes, I am."

"Good heavens, so you must be Joe and Eve's boy."

Norman's jaw dropped. "You know about me then?"

"Only since your father died," admitted Lottie, "before that we knew nothing about the Old Bakehouse or its history. We hadn't even heard of Joe."

The sisters then proceeded to tell Norman how his mother had left his father allegedly for someone else when he was just a little boy of two and how after their departure Joe never baked another loaf again and eventually went to work at Pentrillick House.

"So did he continue to live in the Old Bakehouse?" Jackie asked.

Hetty nodded. "Yes, he died there in fact and was discovered by Karen and Nicki who work in the hairdressing salon next door. They knew something was wrong because his little dog kept barking. They went inside and found him dead in his bed."

"So he died in his sleep," sighed Norman, "at least that's a nice way to go."

Jackie looked alarmed. "What happened to the little dog?"

"I'm not sure," admitted Hetty, "Perhaps someone from the solicitors' office is looking after him until a new home can be found."

"I heard it was one of the executors," said Lottie, "whoever they might be."

Jackie looked at her next door neighbour. "Well whatever, you must have him, Norman. It'll be nice for you to have company now your mum's gone."

"Yeah, maybe. I'll look into it although I doubt if Muffins will be impressed and really it might be best if the poor dog stayed in the village."

"Muffins?" queried Hetty.

"Norman's cat," Jackie replied.

"I see."

"So going back to your family, I assume your mother came from down here," surmised Lottie.

Norman nodded. "Yes, that's right. Her maiden name was Johns."

"Any idea if she had any siblings and if so might they still be living?"

"She had a sister called Alice who I believe was the younger of the two. They weren't close, in fact as far as I know they've not seen each other for donkey's years and I've never even met her. They did exchange Christmas cards though and Aunt Alice used to send me money for my birthday when I was young. I believe she's still alive because Mum definitely had a card from her last Christmas."

"Really! Any idea where your aunt lives?" Lottie asked.

"Yes, in Porthleven wherever that might be."

"Porthleven, that's near Helston so not far from here."

"In which case I suppose I ought to look her up and tell her that Mum's dead because no-one else will have told her."

"She might like to come to your dad's funeral as well," suggested Jackie, thoughtfully, "after all, years ago Joe would have been her brother-in-law."

"By the looks of it he still was 'til the day he died because Mum and Joe were never divorced: of that I'm one hundred percent certain."

Chapter Four

On Monday afternoon the church in Pentrillick filled up rapidly as mourners gathered to bid farewell to the village's oldest resident; after the service they made their way to the Crown and Anchor where the executors of Joe's will had made arrangements for a buffet to be laid on. However, before Norman and Jackie left the churchyard they looked along the rows of graves hoping to find the final resting place for Joe's parents and any other members of the Williams family from back along. It was Jackie who found their graves alongside a drystone wall. While Norman slowly read the inscriptions on his grandparents' tombstones, Jackie looked further along the row. When she spotted another grave marked Williams she stopped and then called out to Norman. "This must be where your father's younger brother is buried. The one Hetty and Lottie told us about who was killed during the war when he was just a teenager."

"And he'd have been my uncle, not that I would ever have known him even if we'd have stayed here as he died quite a few years before I was born." Norman sighed. "I wonder what he was like. I wonder what they were all like."

Not far away were the graves of Eve's parents, Betty and Cyril Johns. Norman was overcome with emotion. "Mum's mum and dad. Joe's mum and dad, all buried here and I never knew any of them. Or at least I did when a tot but being just two when we left I don't remember them. I can't believe that my roots are here in a village which until a few days ago I'd never even heard of. I feel quite moved by it all but it's nice in a way because it gives me a sense of belonging."

Jackie linked her arm through his. "Don't be miserable, Norm. I'm sure your mum had her reasons for leaving and although we'll probably never know what they were I'm sure she had your best interest at heart."

"Yes, I suppose so but why did she never tell me the truth? I can understand as a child but not in these recent years. And why didn't she tell me after Oscar died? I mean he wasn't my dad but she let me go on believing he was."

"I suppose she didn't want to upset you," Jackie chuckled. "Anyway, whatever, you can say with hand on heart that you're a Cornishman now. You couldn't say that a few weeks ago."

That made Norman smile. "Yes, both my parents were Cornish so I really am a Cornishman. Fancy that. I'd better start practising the accent."

He noticed Jackie wince when he attempted the dialect. "Okay, perhaps not then."

As they walked away from the graves of Eve's parents they passed by an area where small headstones, close together and relatively new, predominantly occupied a patch of ground.

Norman stopped walking. "This must be where peoples' ashes are buried. "Do you think Mum would like it if I brought her here? After all this is where she came from and her parents are here."

"I think that's a lovely idea. Much better than her being on the shelf in your pantry."

Norman chuckled. "Yes, not the best of places to rest. I must have a word with the vicar if he's in the pub. I can't see as there would be any objections because her roots are here and she was married in this church. Probably even baptised here too. Joe might not be too glad to see her back though but this spot is quite a distance from where he's buried so if they were prone to argue a lot they'll be far enough apart."

Inside the Crown and Anchor, Hetty, Lottie, their friend, Debbie, and Kitty sat around a table near to the piano sipping wine and discussing the funeral. "I suppose Norman will be entitled to proceeds from the sale of the Old Bakehouse," Kitty glanced at the door as he entered the bar with Jackie, "after all I don't think he has any other living relatives."

"We did mention that to him," said Hetty, "but he seemed reluctant to do anything about it. He said if his father chose to leave him anything then he'd be grateful but he wasn't prepared to poke his nose in as Joe may well have left everything to someone he's not aware of. What's more, Norman doesn't think Joe knew where he and Eve were living as there had never been any correspondence between him and his mother. Not that he's aware of anyway."

"So, is Norman paying for the funeral?" Debbie glanced across the bar to where Norman and Jackie were now chatting to Vicar Sam.

Lottie shook her head. "No, he looked into it apparently and was told by the solicitors handling the will that payment will come out of the estate."

"I wonder which solicitors are handling it," Kitty mused.

"You know who they are but I can't remember what they're called," said Hetty, "Remember, they have an office in Penzance where Kyle works."

"Of course, silly me. That's how you got to know who the estate agents were."

"That's right and hopefully Kyle will be able to give us a few updates as regards the will."

Lottie tutted. "No he won't, Het. That really would be out of order."

Kitty looked around at the people gathered. "Is Norman's aunt here? You said he was going to tell her about the funeral."

Hetty shook her head. "Sadly not. He and Jackie went to see her on Saturday but apparently she has a nasty cough and so didn't want to ruin the service which is understandable. Norman said they didn't stay long because it was hard for her to talk and he didn't want Jackie to catch the cold but he's promised to come back to Cornwall again soon and see her then. I think they got on quite well so it'll be nice for him to know that he actually has a living family member down here."

"Who is that young woman with Norman?" Kitty nodded towards Jackie, "I mean, surely she's not his girlfriend."

Hetty smothered a smile. "No, of course not. Apparently, they live next door to each other and Jackie, that's her name, used to pop in and help Norman with his mother Eve in the last few months of her life. She lives with her parents and the families have always got on well. Jackie told us she's known Norman for quite a few years now."

"So if Norman and his late mother live next door to Jackie, and Norman and Jackie are neighbours, does that mean Norman still lived with his parents until his mum died?" Debbie asked.

Hetty laughed. "You make it sound really confusing, but yes, that's right."

"So Norman has never married?"

"No, and as he's sixty-two now it looks like he's a confirmed bachelor."

"Seems a bit odd to still be living with his parents when in his sixties though, don't you think?" Debbie recalled how she had craved independence when several decades younger than Norman.

"Well I suppose if they all got on alright there wouldn't have been any reason for him to move away and Norman's father, or should I say the man he always thought was his father, died several years ago anyway." Hetty laughed, "What's more, he probably didn't want to forgo his mum's cooking."

"So when did his mum die? Eve I think you said her name was."

"Yes, she was Eve and she died a few weeks back."

Debbie tutted. "Well whatever, I think it was very cruel of this Eve woman never to have told Norman who his real father was."

Hetty nodded. "I'm inclined to agree because had she done so Joe and Norman could have met up. Kitty reckons they're quite alike in looks and manner, don't you Kitty?"

"Very much so and of course I knew Joe when he was the same age as Norman."

"Poor Joe," sighed Debbie, thinking of the erstwhile baker, "So he died all alone knowing that he had a son out there somewhere but he knew nothing of his whereabouts or even if he was still alive."

"He also had another child," Lottie reminded them, "don't forget about the baby born to his first wife who was adopted when a few weeks old."

"Good point," acknowledged Hetty, "I wonder if he or she knows anything of his or her biological parents."

When the October edition of the *Pentrillick Gazette* came out, villagers were astounded to read an announcement by the executors of Joe Williams' will. It read as follows –

We, the executors of the last will and testament of the late Joseph Percival Williams hereby let it be known as instructed by said Joseph Percival Williams that one calendar month after a buyer has begun proceedings to purchase the Old Bakehouse, Pentrillick in the County of Cornwall, that an advertisement shall be placed in the Pentrillick Gazette and other local newspapers requesting all offspring of said Joseph Percival Williams, be they legitimate or illegitimate, put forth their names to partake in a share of the final sum, after expenses, raised from the sale of the Old Bakehouse and other monies included in the estate. Applicants shall be required to take a DNA test to prove authenticity. As instructed the closing date for claims shall be at midnight on the last day of the month, approximately six weeks after completion of sale; therefore, said date and time is to be midnight on the thirtieth day of November 2018. Applicants must apply in person to Tremayne, Watts and Braithwaite, Solicitors, Trevithick Rd. Penzance.

Signed – Alexander W Copeland. (Executor) Hillside, Blackberry Way, Pentrillick, Cornwall.
Virginia G Copeland. (Executor) Hillside, Blackberry Way, Pentrillick, Cornwall.

"So our next door neighbours are the executors!" Lottie exclaimed, after the sisters had read the article, "Fancy that."

Hetty looked puzzled. "Are they?" Her expression changed as the penny dropped. "Oh, yes of course, I didn't look at the addresses. Alexander and Virginia will be Alex and Ginny. Well, I never. I suppose they knew Joe because their antiques shop is only a few doors away from the Old Bakehouse."

"And now you come to mention it, I've heard a dog barking next door, so Alex and Ginny must be looking after Joe's dog for the time being." Lottie was surprised she had not realised this before.

"Anyway, it's exciting," chuckled Hetty, rubbing her hands together, "because we might be able to wheedle some information out of them. We know how much the Old Bakehouse is selling for but not how much Joe had in the bank. I mean, he could well have accrued quite a substantial amount over the years."

Lottie tutted. "Don't be daft, Het. They'll not tell you anything. Alex is as straight as the day is long."

As details of the announcement sank in a small number of Pentrillick's residents began to question their parentage and to look in mirrors hopeful of seeing a resemblance between their own images and those of the late Joseph Percival Williams whose photograph accompanied the announcement in the *Pentrillick Gazette.*

"We could well be inundated with people when word of the advertisement gets more widespread," said Hetty, as she sat down in the Crown and Anchor one Tuesday evening after bingo. "I see there are quite a few unfamiliar faces in here already tonight."

"I was thinking along the same lines," Debbie removed her coat and placed it behind her back, "Can't blame folks for trying though. Not when there's a few bob a stake."

Lottie handed out the drinks and opened a packet of crisps which she placed in the centre of the table to share with her sister and Debbie. "Anyway, it's nice to know Norman will get something."

"Probably the whole lot even," reasoned Hetty, "and it'd be well deserved if he did."

"Do you think we ought to try and let him know so that he can apply?" Lottie asked.

Hetty shook he head. "No, he was in touch with the solicitors when he was down here so they already know about him."

"Of course. Silly me."

"They probably even told him about the forthcoming advert but asked him not to tell anyone," suggested Debbie.

"It's a pity they invented this DNA thing," grumbled Hetty, "because if they hadn't we could have interrogated the claimants ourselves to see if we thought their cases were legitimate."

Lottie laughed. "I don't think we'd qualify for that job, Het. It'd have to be done by a legal team whether DNA was available or not. And if we did partake in the investigations it's unlikely we'd be able to wheedle out the truth especially as we've only known the village for a couple of years and so don't have much knowledge of folks from back-along."

Debbie giggled. "You're right, Lottie. In fact none of us at this table even knew old Joe or anything about him until a week or so ago."

"Still be nice to try," sighed Hetty, dreamily, "and it'd be interesting to have something to do as we approach the dark days of winter."

"Well, why don't we have a go?" Debbie asked, "There's nothing to stop us grilling the applicants subtly even if our investigations wouldn't be any help to the authorities."

"But how can you grill someone subtly?" Lottie chuckled, "They'd soon smell a rat. Besides how would we know who to grill? I mean, they're hardly likely to wear badges telling of their applications."

Hetty waved her hand towards the bar. "That shouldn't be a problem with Tess working here. She'll be able to point us in the direction of any likely candidates and we'll soon get them chatting, especially if any are women."

"That's if they come to Pentrillick in the first place," reasoned Debbie, "it might be that most will get no nearer than the solicitor's office in Penzance."

"They're bound to come here," insisted Hetty, "because they'll want to see where it all began and peer in the windows of the Old Bakehouse. Not that they'll see much with the old net curtains blocking the view."

A week later there was much excitement in Pentrillick for, the previous day, Tess Dobson who worked part-time as a barmaid at the Crown and Anchor, let it be known to all and sundry that a television crew from the South West were to visit the village on Wednesday to film a report about Joe Williams' will and then afterwards they were to have lunch in the pub and had booked tables in advance.

"I wonder what time they're filming," gushed Hetty, when Kitty called round to tell them the news which she had just learned while in the post office.

"It's got to be in the morning," reasoned Lottie, "If they're having lunch in the pub afterwards."

"Good thinking. We'll have to get up bright and early on Wednesday then because we don't want to miss anything and I'll need time to plan what to wear?"

"What to wear!" Lottie laughed, "They're not going to be filming you, you muppet."

"No, but I might just happen to be in the background somewhere and I should hate to look a mess."

The main street in Pentrillick was far busier than usual on Wednesday morning and more reminiscent of a sunny day at the height of the holiday season than that of a drab day in October. People wearing their Sunday best tried to look natural as they peered in shop windows, stood outside the church on pretence of reading the notice board and chatted in groups as though having bumped into each other by chance. Meanwhile, many who lived along the street decided it was the perfect day to clean their windows despite the grey clouds looming with the threat of rain; others swept up leaves from their front garden paths and some even washed their cars.

Hetty, Lottie, Debbie and Kitty were amongst the villagers. Their chosen spot was outside the hairdressers where they planned to speak in loud stage whispers about going inside to make hair appointments. The reason for their choice being that it was of course next door to the Old Bakehouse which was sure to feature in the television report.

The television crew arrived in due course and while discussing where the presenter should stand and so forth, Hetty, Lottie, Debbie and Kitty having performed their rehearsed conversation slipped into the hairdressers and watched from the window as the presenter's make-up was touched up and everything was put in place. Peering into the street beside them stood hairdressers, Karen and Nicki, along with two customers quite happy to leave the chairs where their hair was being styled in order to look outside and join in the excitement.

"You ought to go out there, Lottie," urged Kitty, "You could tell them it's your son who is buying the Old Bakehouse. It might interest them."

The colour rose in Lottie's cheeks. "No way am I doing that. I'd die of embarrassment."

"It's a good idea though," Hetty agreed, "I think you should do it."

"Yes, go on, Lottie," urged Debbie, "then we can watch you on tonight's news."

"No," Lottie was emphatic.

"Coward," tutted Hetty.

"You go then, Het," said Karen, "after all Bill is your nephew and you know as much about the place as Lottie."

"Oh…yes, I suppose he is but…"

"You suppose," blurted Debbie, "of course he's your nephew."

"Yes, but…"

"Now who's a coward?" mocked Lottie.

"Coward!" Hetty stood up straight. "Are you calling me a coward?"

"Yes," the ladies all replied.

"Okay, in which case I'll do it."

And to the amazement of the others, Hetty left the salon head held high and casually approached the television crew. In her best telephone voice she told them that it was her nephew, Bill, who was in the throes of purchasing the Old Bakehouse and how hairdressers, Karen and Nicki had discovered Joe's body. As she spoke a few spots of rain fell from the heavens.

"Quick get a few shots of the Old Bakehouse," commanded the woman who appeared to be in charge, "and we'll film the rest in the hairdressers. That's if they'll let us."

And so that evening when the broadcast went out, viewers saw a brief glimpse of the Old Bakehouse exterior; the rest was filmed inside the hairdressing salon, where Hetty and Lottie as instructed by the film crew, pretended to be at the desk booking hair appointments where they told of their family connection with the adjacent building. The next interview was with Karen and Nicki who continued to style the hair of the real customers as they told how they found Joe through his dog. Meanwhile, Kitty sat beside the wash basins in pretence of waiting to have her hair washed and Debbie, with hurriedly put in curlers bulging beneath a hairnet, sat under a buzzing hair dryer and turned the pages of a glossy magazine.

Chapter Five

With time on their hands while they patiently waited for the sale of the Old Bakehouse to be concluded, Hetty and Lottie decided to visit Norman's Aunt Alice in Porthleven keen to learn anything they could about the last occupants of the property, because until Bill and Sandra had the keys there was no chance of them having a look round the old building and conjuring up a picture of its past for themselves.

They found the elderly lady alone in her cottage; like her nephew Norman, she was tall but in contrast she was lean. The sisters introduced themselves and briefly explained how they had recently met her nephew, Norman in the Crown and Anchor.

"Yes, yes, I remember he did mention you and said that you might call. Please come in." She stepped back for them to enter her home. "Now tell me, have I got this right? You are the ladies related to the people purchasing the Old Bakehouse in Pentrillick?"

"That's right," Lottie confirmed, as she wiped her feet on the door mat, "It's my son Bill and his wife Sandra who are buying it."

"Any children?" Alice asked.

"Three. Zac who is eighteen and twin girls, Kate and Vicki who are sixteen."

"Oh good, it'll be lovely for the house to have youngsters there. It's been a long time since there were any." Alice closed the front door and then looked at the sisters more closely. "Are you the pair that were on the local news the other day in the hairdressers?"

Hetty beamed, "Yes."

Lottie looked embarrassed.

"Well I never. Not often I get celebrities come and visit."

Lottie winced. "Are you feeling better now?" she asked, as they followed Alice into her cosy sitting room where a log fire crackled in the hearth.

"Yes, thank you, dear but I'm still a bit croaky. I hate coughs they're such an inconvenience and I really would have liked to have attended Joe's funeral for old time's sake. Please take a seat." The sisters sat down on the sofa.

"It was a lovely service and the turnout was impressive too." Lottie pulled out an order of service card from her handbag and showed it to Alice who took it as she sat down in the chair nearest the fire.

"Can you leave this for a while and then I can put my specs on and look at it at my leisure."

"You can keep it. Hetty has one so we don't need both and to be fair we didn't even know Joe and only went to the funeral because of the bakehouse connection."

"I see, thank you," Alice propped the card behind a framed photograph of a handsome young man. "I wonder what happened to Joe's possessions."

"At the moment they're all still in the house," Lottie disclosed, "You see, to save the expense of the solicitors finding someone to clear it out, Bill said to leave it all and he and Sandra will do it instead."

"They'll have plenty of time," Hetty added, "because they'll stay with us for a while until the place is modernised, decorated and so forth."

"Well in that case if your family find any old photos amongst his things please ask them not to throw them away because I'm sure Norman would like to see them."

Feeling warm, Hetty unbuttoned her jacket. "Don't worry we've already discussed that so all personal and knick-knacky things will be put aside for him to go through."

Alice glanced up at a cuckoo clock on the wall above the fireplace, "Would you like a cup of coffee? I see it's nearly eleven and I usually have a cup then."

"That would be very nice but we don't want to put you to any trouble," said Lottie.

"It's no trouble but perhaps you'd come with me to the kitchen and help me carry it through. Save loading up a tray."

"Of course."

While in the kitchen they heard the cuckoo signal it was eleven o'clock. Hetty looked disappointed. "Bad timing there, I should like to have seen the cuckoo in action."

Alice laughed. "Don't worry, he'll put in an appearance again at half past eleven, albeit just the once."

When the coffee was made and they were back seated around the fire Alice asked, "Have you been inside the Old Bakehouse yet?"

Lottie shook her head. "No, but my son and his wife have of course and they love it. We're told it has huge potential and a lovely olde worlde feel."

"And a whopping great inglenook fireplace in the sitting room apparently," Hetty added.

"Well I suppose it would have an olde worlde feel," smiled Alice, "because it must be one of the oldest buildings in the village."

"Yes, someone did say that to us," Hetty recalled.

"And I assume you remember the days when bread was baked there," said Lottie.

"Oh yes, of course. I remember when Joe had two new electric ovens installed as well. They were his pride and joy and made life so much easier. The old stone oven was lovely but it wasn't so easy to control the temperature as it is with the flick of a switch."

"Sandra, my daughter-in-law, said something about exposing the old oven to make it a feature because they intend to convert the baking room into a kitchen."

Alice put her head to one side as she tried to visualise the old oven. "If I remember correctly the stonework was quite attractive but I'm not sure it'd be my idea of a nice feature. To be honest I prefer to see stonework on the outside of a house and like interior walls to be smooth and washable, especially in the kitchen but then different generations like different things and quite rightly too."

Lottie smiled. "And if I'm honest I'd have to agree with you, Alice."

Hetty was non-committal.

"So would you like to hear a little of the Old Bakehouse's history?"

"Yes please," replied the sisters in unison.

"And the people who lived there," Hetty added. "We're intrigued to know what they were like."

"Well, I can't tell you a great deal because after Eve left I'm sure I never went there again. I was married soon after, you see, and my late husband and I moved here to Porthleven so there was no need to go to Pentrillick and Joe had closed the bakery anyway. This is my husband by the way." She pointed to the photograph behind which she had placed the Order of Service sheet. "Taken many years ago I might add."

"He was very handsome," said Lottie. Hetty nodded to agree.

"Yes, and he was still handsome when in the autumn of his years. Bless him."

"So when exactly did Eve leave?" Hetty asked, "We believe it was when Norman was two years old."

"That's right he was. Now let me think. If he was two it would've been 1958. Yes, definitely 1958 and it was in January

I believe. Yes, yes of course it was January because it was a few days after my eighteenth birthday. Not that I came of age then like they do now. Back then you had to wait until you were twenty one to get the key of the door."

"Ah, yes," chuckled Hetty, "the law changed in 1970 and as Lottie and I were born in 1952 we were some of the first to benefit from the change, if there were any benefits other than being able to marry without parents' consent and being able to vote."

"Well to be able to marry without parents' consent is a blessing as far as I'm concerned. I was eighteen, you see, when I got wed which meant I had to ask my parents' permission. Mum was fine about it but Dad wasn't…miserable so-and-so. I got my way in the end though."

"You must have missed your sister when she went," sympathised Lottie, "especially with her having gone up-county. I can't imagine being separated from Het by more than a few miles."

"Yes, I did miss her for a while but at the same time I was angry with her. I considered Joe to be a good man, you see. Admittedly, he was a bit of a flirt but I thought it very wrong of Eve to have taken Norman away from his father. And as regards missing her, I had plenty to occupy my time with a new husband, a new house and so forth."

"So, when did you last see her?"

Alice hung her head. "I'm ashamed to say it was sixty years ago and the day before she left. After she went she wrote to me saying where she was but asked me not to tell Joe or his elderly parents. And so I never saw her again. We kept in touch by post but our letters were very few and far between. Just birthdays and Christmas I suppose."

Hetty cast a quizzical glance in Alice's direction. "If you saw Eve the day before she left surely she must behaved differently or said something which might have given you a clue as to her imminent departure?"

"No, there was no indication whatsoever. She behaved like she always did which in retrospect I've always considered to be a little odd."

Hetty tutted. "How strange, it must have been a great shock to you then when Norman called here."

A huge smile crept across Alice's face and then she laughed. "It was and at first I thought I was seeing a ghost. He looks so much like Joe, you see. Older of course than the young baker I remember but his face has the same expression and his blue eyes, well, they're one and the same."

"I take it that you liked Joe." Hetty found Alice's chuckle to be infectious.

"Yes, I did. Everyone did. He'd lived in the village all his life so was known by all. I remember he was a keen gardener at one time and grew his own vegetables as well as flowers. He loved the birds too and fed them every day during the winter. Robins were his favourites but he loved them all, big and small. Yes, so all in all he was a good chap and we got on well despite the fact he was twenty one years older than me," Alice smiled, "and so in a way he was more of a father figure than a brother-in-law."

"Hmm, quite an age gap then."

"Yes, he was older than Eve as well by sixteen years but no-one would ever have guessed. Eve was old for her years and Joe very young at heart and I like to think he was until the day he died."

"Did you ever meet Joe's first wife?" Hetty asked.

"I remember her vaguely but I was only four when she died. I believe her name was Cicely and she and Joe met and married during the war. I don't know where the wedding took place but it was in a registry office somewhere or other up-country. Of course because she didn't come from Cornwall no-one knew her family."

"What about your parents?" Hetty asked, "How did they take Eve running off with their grandson and allegedly another man?"

"They took it better than me. At least my father did. Mum was pretty upset because she liked Joe. She was a keen gardener too, you see. They kept in touch with Eve for a while and even talked of visiting her and Norman but they never did. Mum's health deteriorated and she died soon after and then within a year Dad was dead too. He fell from a ladder, banged his head, knocked himself unconscious and died two days later from his injuries."

"Oh dear, I am sorry," commiserated Lottie.

Alice shrugged her shoulders. "Don't be, it was a long time ago and Dad wasn't the kindest of men. To tell you the truth he made my life a misery at times. As I said earlier, he tried to stop me getting married."

Lottie thought it best not to respond.

"How about Joe's parents?" Hetty asked, "How did it affect them?"

"They were both very frail and I got the impression they were glad to see the back of Eve. They were a nice couple and to try and keep the peace I went to see them shortly after she left but I never went back again. I suppose I should have but I didn't feel welcome. They didn't even offer me a cup of tea. Hardly surprising really." Alice looked genuinely remorseful. "Still, it's all water under the bridge and we can't turn the clock back, can we?"

Hetty shook her head. "Sadly not."

"Anyway, that's enough about me and my family. Tell about yourselves. I can tell from your accents that you're not Cornish so have you been here long and what brought you down here?"

Glad to see that Alice was smiling again, Hetty and Lottie told her about their holiday in 2016. How they had enjoyed it; fallen in love with the area and then moved to Pentrillick just before Christmas that same year.

Chapter Six

On Friday the twenty sixth of October, the sale of Bill and Sandra's house in Northamptonshire and the purchase of the Old Bakehouse were completed and in the early evening as darkness fell the family arrived in Pentrillick shortly after the removal van containing all their worldly goods. Because the removal van was parked on the main street in front of the house, Bill parked round the corner in Goose Lane near to the side gate which led into the garden of their new home.

As the family were not going to live in the house until certain work was completed their furniture was quickly stacked inside the downstairs rooms along with the sparse amounts of furniture which had belonged to old Joe. When the removal men left, the family had a brief look round the house, especially the children who were seeing it for the first time.

"It's dark, cold and creepy," Kate folded her arms tightly to keep warm, "especially with the moon shining in the windows but I think I like it."

Bill put his arm around her shoulder. "Don't worry, Kate. Once we get the place cleaned up, decorated and heated and have our furniture spread out it'll soon feel like home."

"Can we choose our own rooms?" Vicki asked, as she looked up the stairs.

"Of course," said Sandra, "but the biggest room on the front is already taken. It's for me and your dad."

"And try and do it without arguing," Bill called as Vicki and Zac raced up the stairs. Kate, however, held back.

"Don't you want to choose your room?" Sandra asked.

Kate bit her bottom lip. "Yes, but I was just thinking. Which room did old Joe die in?"

"The biggest, first door on the right which as I just said is the room we're having," laughed Bill, "It must have been Joe's because his clothes are in the wardrobe there and his slippers are still under the bed. The other rooms are smaller and don't look like anyone's slept in them for years."

Kate's face lit up. "Wait for me," she shouted as she ran up the stairs to join her sister and brother. Five minutes later the children joined their parents where Sandra was taking a kettle, mugs, teabags, sugar, a tea towel and teaspoons from a washing-up bowl in the kitchenette.

"All done," shrieked Vicki, "I'm having the room next to you on the front with the babies cot in it, Kate's having the one next to the bathroom on the back and Zac wants the L shaped room at the end of the landing."

"Not that I could really see much of it," admitted Zac, "there's no light bulb in there so I had to use my phone to see it."

Sandra placed the emptied washing-up bowl in the sink. "I'm not surprised the bulb's gone. Judging by the dust I should imagine Joe never used half of the house."

"Anyway, I'm impressed," said Bill, "you chose your rooms without falling out."

Sandra agreed. "And if you've seen enough I suggest we get off to Primrose Cottage because I don't know about you lot but I'm feeling cold and I'm dying to sit by a fire with a cup of tea."

"Can we come back and have a proper look tomorrow when it's light?" Kate asked as they left the building.

"Of course," Bill locked the door, "and no doubt Grandma and Auntie Hetty will want to come and have a look as well."

As they walked round the corner into Goose Lane, Sandra glanced up at the rooftops; perched on a chimney pot and framed by a full moon was a large black bird. She pointed to the chimney and shuddered. "That's not a very good omen."

Bill laughed. "And how pray is a poor old crow a bad omen?"

"It's not a crow it's a raven and ravens are harbingers of death."

"Looks like a crow to me."

"Well, it's not. Ravens are bigger than crows and they're scruffier too."

"Well that little fellow's certainly scruffy." Bill dropped the house keys into his pocket and took out the car keys.

"I reckon it's a rook," joked Zac.

"Or a jackdaw," giggled Vicki.

Kate looked nervous. "Mum, why do you say ravens are harbingers of death?"

Sandra shrugged her shoulders. "Not sure really but they are and it's also believed that witches can transform themselves into ravens so they can fly away to avoid being captured. That's if you believe in witches."

Bill laughed as he unlocked the car. "Where did you read that load of cobblers?"

"I didn't read it. I was told it by my granny. It's a part of Welsh mythology."

"But your granny wasn't Welsh: she was a Brummie."

"On Dad's side yes, but Mum's mother was Welsh and so was her father. It's a pity they'd passed away before I met you because you would have liked them."

"Hmm," Bill slipped into the driving seat but thought it best not to comment.

The following morning, the family were up bright and early as were Hetty and Lottie. All were eager to explore the Old Bakehouse thoroughly in daylight and because the morning was dry and sunny and there were no grey clouds in the sky, they walked down Long Lane into the village rather than take the cars.

As they approached the house Bill glanced up to the rooftops. "Oh thank goodness, it looks like the scruffy crow's gone. Perhaps he only comes out in moonlight."

"Don't start that again, William," snapped Sandra.

Hetty frowned. "William? You never call Bill, William."

"She does when she's mad with him," giggled Vicki.

Lottie looked at the roof. "What's all this about a crow?"

"Take no notice," said Sandra, "Bill's just being impish."

"There was a bird on the roof last night and Mum said it was a raven and that they're harbingers of death," blurted Kate. "She also said some creepy stuff about witches."

Sandra felt her cheeks redden; the words she had spoken the previous evening seemed very silly on a bright sunny morning.

Bill chuckled as he unlocked the door. "It's Welsh mythology apparently and Sandra was told it by her Welsh granny."

"Well there could be something in it," reasoned Hetty, "after all Joe died here not long ago."

"Quite right," agreed Lottie, "it could mean there's to be another death, they go in threes and we've learned of two recently connected with the Old Bakehouse."

"Two?" Sandra queried.

Lottie nodded. "Yes, Joe and Eve."

"That's quite enough about death and ravens I think." Bill was aware of the horrified look on Kate's face, "Anyway, I still say it was a scruffy crow."

As they entered the house and stepped into the room which would originally have been the shop, Kate's expression changed. "Wow, it looks so much nicer in daytime with the sun shining in."

Vicki agreed. "And friendlier too. I'm going up to see my room."

"So am I," Zac was eager to see his room in daylight.

"First impressions?" Bill asked his mother and aunt.

"I like it," Lottie inhaled, "It has a nice homely feel to it and doesn't smell as musty as I thought it would."

"Will you be using this as a dining room?" Hetty asked, seeing the Formica topped table and four chairs in the centre of the room.

"Yes, but with our own table and chairs. I think these have seen better days and will probably end up in the garden or the outhouse." Sandra rocked the back of a chair to demonstrate its fragility.

Hetty's eyes were drawn towards a small bookcase. "Alice said that Joe was fond of birds and the books here confirm it. They're the subject of all the ones on the top shelf."

"And by the sound of things he wasn't just fond of the feathered variety," chuckled Bill.

Sandra tutted. "Come on, let's show you the rest of the house." She led the way into the hall off which ran the large sitting room crammed with furniture. When Hetty spotted a piano standing in a corner her face lit up. "That's my old piano, isn't it? I'd forgotten all about it."

"Yes, it is and look over there." Sandra pointed to the opposite side of the room where another piano stood.

"Well, I'll be blowed. So did Joe play, I wonder." Hetty approached the piano, lifted the lid and struck a few notes. It was hopelessly out of tune.

"Well, if he did he obviously hadn't played for a while," chuckled Bill.

"And you'd be more than welcome to have your old piano back," said Sandra, "Kate doesn't play much now so one will be more than enough."

"Or you can have Joe's if you'd rather," suggested Bill, "it looks quite fancy."

"I'll certainly have one of them. I've still got the electric keyboard I bought but it just isn't the same."

After they left the sitting room they went upstairs to see the four bedrooms and the bathroom.

"My goodness, look at that cot," cried Hetty as they stepped inside Vicki's room, "It's real nineteen fifties. What will you do with it?"

Vicki answered before either of her parents had a chance to reply, "I'd like to keep it and then I can put all my old dolls and teddies in it. I'll paint it first though and in a colour to match my room when it's decorated."

Bill was impressed. "Well done, it's good to see you planning ahead."

"I suppose Norman must have slept in it when he was a baby," smiled Lottie, as they moved on to the next room, "I must admit that does rather stretch the imagination."

After viewing all the bedrooms they peeped inside the bathroom and then turned back towards the stairs.

"I like the house very much but it needs quite a lot of work done to it," said Lottie, as they reached the lower hallway.

"Yes, it does," Bill agreed, "but it's structurally sound so much of it is just cosmetic. Main things to be done are modernising the bathroom, getting central heating installed and turning the old baking room into a kitchen."

"And getting a wood burner fitted," Sandra added.

"So where is the old baking room?" Lottie asked as they stepped back into the dining room.

"Through here." Sandra led the small party into the kitchenette and then into the baking room.

"Wow, it's huge," Hetty did a twirl and then gazed up at the beams.

"And this wall here," Sandra said, pointing to the large chimney breast, "is the one we told you about that we intend to expose. There should be a nice bit of granite behind the plaster and probably the old oven and if so that'll be a nice feature."

Lottie opened the back door. "A porch and a big one at that. It'll be handy for boots shoes and so forth."

"It will and we think we might have the central heating boiler out there as well," said Bill.

"The washing machine too," Sandra added, "and if it's possible we'd like to have a downstairs loo fitted. There's enough room."

"What's in there?" Hetty pointed to the outbuilding visible from the porch window.

"Junk," said Sandra, "which Bill is longing to rummage through."

As she spoke there was a knock on the front door. Bill answered; on the doorstep stood Basil a builder who had recently done a loft conversion for Hetty and Lottie, and with him was Sid the plumber. They had been invited to see what work needed to be done. After they had looked over the property and weighed up the situation, Sandra made tea for everyone and they went into the dining room where some sat on the four chairs and the rest stood.

"So any idea when you'll be able to make a start?" Bill eagerly asked Basil and Sid.

Basil scratched his chin. "I've got a job I need to finish next week and then the week after I was due to convert a garage into living space but the lady who I'd be doing it for has been taken ill so that's put on hold. So I see no reason why I shouldn't be able to start here then instead."

Sid nodded. "Me too, because lots of my jobs are just a day's work so I can fit you in to run alongside everyone else. I assume you'll want the bathroom done first."

"Splendid," Sandra clapped her hands with glee, "and yes, Sid, the bathroom must have priority because the water heater over the bath looks ready to drop and we prefer showers anyway. And then next priority will have to be installing central heating because the house feels very cold and damp at the moment."

"Well, if you can both start that soon," said Bill. "Next week we'll pull together and get as much furniture as we can out of the baking room, and then we'll start going through old Joe's stuff and see what to keep and what to dispose of."

"Can we help sort things out?" Hetty eagerly asked.

"Of course, the more the merrier."

As he spoke there was another knock on the door.

"Emma, lovely to see you dear." Sandra kissed her son's friend on the cheek.

"Zac messaged me last night and said I must come and see your new house."

"Of course," Sandra stepped back to let Emma in. "Needless to say it's a mess at the moment but I think everyone likes it."

Hearing Emma's voice, Zac appeared from the sitting room. He gave her a hug and then showed her around the house.

"So, what are you doing now you've finished your college course?" Sandra asked Emma, as they stood in the kitchenette drinking coffee after her tour of the house, "If I remember correctly you were studying tourism or something like that."

"That's right, hospitality and tourism and now I'm working at Pentrillick House as a tour guide. I've replaced Cynthia Watkins who retired in September so it's worked out just right."

"Ah, Cynthia with the annoying voice," declared Hetty, "I remember her."

Emma smiled. "Yes, I can see what you mean but she knows the history of the house inside out and helped me a lot in the two months before she retired."

"And I suppose before long the Christmas Wonderland will be up and running gain," said Sandra, "We've not seen it yet so look forward to that."

"You'll love it," Lottie enthused.

"Yes, I'm really enjoying the preparation work for it. Then next year Tristan plans to use the house for events such as weddings and so I'm to be involved with that as well."

Bill nodded. "Very nice, and do you enjoy your work?"

"Very much so. It's not very adventurous of me but I wanted to work as near home as possible so it's ideal and I love it."

"Good, now we need to find Zac a job but at the moment he has no idea what he wants to do."

Emma looked at Zac. "While you're deciding why not go and see Ashley and Alison at the pub, they're always happy to take people on that they know and especially in the run up to Christmas."

"Brilliant, I'll pop down and see them at lunch time and have a game or two of pool while I'm there. Fancy coming with me?"

"You bet. Kyle will most likely be there too as he likes to get in a bit of practice at the weekend."

Over the next few days Hetty, Lottie and Sandra spent their time sorting through Joe's belongings. Bill meanwhile started work with the supermarket chain with whom he had been transferred and the twins began to attend their new school and work towards their A-Levels. Zac, after his visit with Emma to the Crown and Anchor secured a part-time job on the bar to bring in some money while he made up his mind what he wanted to do with his life.

The ladies began their work upstairs in the bedrooms. The unwanted furniture they advertised for free in the post office and on Facebook and to their delight within a couple of days most of it was gone. Joe's clothing they bagged up and took to the charity shop in the village and his personal things they boxed up for Norman. They then took up the old carpets and put them in the outhouse ready for Bill to take to the recycling centre at the weekend. After they had washed the walls and cleaned the windows the upstairs rooms were ready to be decorated and have radiators installed.

"I think we'll leave the sitting room for now," said Sandra, "We can't do much anyway until we've got the beds upstairs."

"Shall we do the kitchenette then?" Lottie asked, "After all you're going to need somewhere to cook and it'll be several weeks before the baking room has been transformed."

As they walked through to the kitchenette, Hetty opened the door of a cupboard under the stairs. "My goodness look at this lot. That'll keep someone busy for a few hours."

Sandra stepped back to take a peep. Inside there were dozens of cardboard boxes, bulging sacks, an ironing board and a vacuum cleaner. "Yes, I think it best if we keep that door shut for now. Out of sight out of mind and all that."

The following Monday, Bill was at work and the twins at school. Inside the Old Bakehouse, Sandra was hanging wallpaper in Kate's bedroom, Sid the plumber was disconnecting the old bathroom suite from the water supply and Basil and his young assistant Mark were working in the old baking room. Zac, eager to make himself useful, restacked boxes, bags and furniture stored in the living room in the space left following the removal of Joe's bits of furniture, and in the kitchenette, Hetty and Lottie made tea and coffee for the workers. When it was ready, Lottie took mugs up to Sid and Sandra while Hetty took mugs to Basil and Mark. Zac fetched his own.

"These ovens look like they've had very little use," commented Basil, as he and Mark pulled the first one away from the wall.

Hetty placed the coffee mugs on the draining board and then ran her fingers along the dusty surface of the ovens. "In which case it looks as though Eve must have run off soon after they were installed because that's when Joe ceased baking. Such a shame. I bet they were beauties in their day."

"What are we going to do with them?" Mark asked.

"I know someone who's going to take them away. Whether or not he'll be able to put them to good use I don't know but I hope he can, otherwise they'll be scrap."

"Such a shame but then we do live in a throwaway society now it seems," Hetty pointed to the chimney breast, "So when will you be starting to expose the old oven, Basil? I must admit I'm curious to see what it'll look like."

"Not today but hopefully tomorrow. The render seems to be a pretty hard mix so I reckon it'll be a full day's work. Besides we want to get these cupboards out first to give us a bit more room."

As they finished their tea, Sid called from the bathroom upstairs. "Can someone come up and help me bring the old bath tub down?"

"I can, but I need to secure this strip of wallpaper first." Sandra was in the next room.

"No need, Mum," Zac ran up the stairs two at a time, "I'll give Sid a hand."

After the bath tub was outside in the back garden, Zac helped Sid carry down the old toilet, cistern and wash basin.

"What now?" he asked when they returned to the empty room.

"The radiator," said Sid, "I need to get that on the wall over there where your mum's painted it white and then get some pipe work done ready for when the chap comes to install the boiler at the end of the week. But before that though we'll get the new loo in to save the ladies having to pop next door to the hairdressers."

"Can I help?"

"Of course, it'll save my back a bit. You'll find the radiator for in here out on the landing."

That evening as the family sat by the fire at Primrose Cottage discussing the day's activities, Zac seemed deep in thought.

"Are you alright, son?" Bill asked, "It's just you seem very quiet this evening."

"Probably tired," said Lottie, "he's been helping Sid today."

"A budding plumber, eh?"

"Well, actually I have been thinking about it," admitted Zac, "Sid says he enjoys his work and would hate to be stuck in an office or something like that and I'm much the same. It must be nice too to get out and about and meet people. I think I'd enjoy it. What do you think?"

"You could do a lot worse," reflected Bill, "and people will always need plumbers. Have you asked Sid about training and so forth?"

Zac smiled. "Yes, and he said if I'm really serious he'd be happy to take me on as an apprentice. It'd mean college work as well but I wouldn't have a problem with that."

"Sounds ideal," gushed Sandra, "I'll have a word with Sid in the morning and then look into it a bit deeper."

Chapter Seven

The following morning, Basil and Mark began to chip away at the chimney breast wall where they hoped to reveal the old oven. Sid was up in the bathroom fitting pipes helped by Zac, Sandra was wallpapering one of the bedrooms and Bill who had the day off work was in the outhouse sorting through boxes some of which looked as though they had not been touched for years.

"Gosh, it's a hive of activity this morning," observed Lottie as she popped her head around the old baking room door after she and Hetty had arrived to help.

As she spoke a huge chunk of plaster fell from the wall. "And it's getting a bit dusty in here." Mark flapped his hand and stepped away.

"Nice bit a stonework underneath though," Basil's voice was muffled by the mask he wore, "should look smashing when it's cleaned up and pointed."

Hetty looked over her sister's shoulder. "Hmm, I think we'll leave you to it and get the kettle on."

Waving dust away from their faces, Hetty and Lottie retreated to the kitchenette and closed the door.

Having heard their voices, Sandra came downstairs to greet the sisters. "You must come and see what Bill found while rummaging in the outhouse earlier this morning."

Hetty put the kettle down on the draining board and with Lottie followed Sandra into the sitting room. Leaning against a table leg was an old weather-beaten board saying S. J. Williams & Sons, Bakers. Established in 1729.

Hetty ran her hand across the wooden board. "Good heavens. Is it the original do you think?"

"No idea but isn't it lovely? I've cleaned it up a bit but it could do with another coat of paint and a bit of filler here and there."

"You can't put it outside though, can you?" Lottie reasoned, "Because if you do you'll have all and sundry walking into your dining room thinking it's still a shop."

"That's what Bill said, which is a shame and so we've decided instead to have it hanging somewhere indoors. Probably in here but not above the fireplace because the heat will dry it out too much."

"Has he found anything else of interest out there?" Lottie glanced towards the back gardens through the patio doors.

"Not yet but there's a large metal trunk at the back which he's trying to reach but to get to it he has to move lots of boxes, a stack of wood, a door or two, old garden tools and stuff like that."

"And it'll probably be empty when he does get to it," laughed Hetty.

As she spoke there was a mighty crash as a huge piece of plaster fell from the chimney breast wall.

"Come and have a look, ladies," they heard Basil shout.

Hetty, Lottie and Sandra dashed into the old baking room where through the dust they could see that part of the oven door was revealed.

"How exciting, I do hope it's still intact." Sandra hopped from foot to foot.

Basil chortled. "You're not thinking of using it surely."

"No, no, but it'll be a lovely feature and no other house in the village will have one. I can see it now and it'll compliment the old beams beautifully."

After leaving Basil to continue chipping away at the old oven door, Hetty and Lottie made tea for everyone and took mugs to the rooms where they worked; they then joined Sandra in one of the bedrooms to help with the wallpapering. Mark meanwhile, took a mug of tea out to Bill in the outhouse.

"There's a great big crow on your roof and he was watching me with his beady eyes as I walked out here." Mark placed the mug on a cluttered work bench.

Bill chuckled. "Don't tell Sandra or she'll get all spooked again. The crow was on the chimney pot the other day, you see but she reckoned it was a raven."

"He's not on the chimney pot now, he's on this roof." Mark pointed upwards."

As Bill's eyes followed Mark's hand they heard footsteps shuffling across the tin roof.

"Perhaps he's hungry," said Bill, "which reminds me, aren't the pasties here yet? I'm starving."

"Nope, your missus said they'd be here at one."

Bill looked at his watch and groaned. "One! That's another hour yet. Okay, Mark, and thanks for the tea."

"You're welcome. Anyway, I better get back and help Baz, not that there's much I can do at the minute apart from clear up the mess he's making."

"Has he managed to uncover the old oven door yet?"

"Nearly. Should be done by lunchtime I reckon."

When the oven door was fully exposed Basil called the ladies back down again; as they entered the room, he attempted to open it.

"Oh, that's a pleasant surprise," he remarked as the latch creaked open, "I really thought it'd be jammed after all this time."

Gently he opened the door only to find the inside of the oven was crudely bricked up. "Hmm, looks like I need to do a bit more chipping. Still, it shouldn't take long."

Disappointed, the ladies returned upstairs to their wallpapering and Basil picked up his tools and began to chip away at the bricks; soon after there was a hole large enough to see a cardboard box on the other side. Basil called the ladies back downstairs and they were joined by Sid and Zac. The excitement amongst the onlookers grew and Bill, thinking the noise meant the pasties had arrived, joined everyone else. When all of the bricks were removed they all huddled around the oven door where the cardboard box tied up with string was clearly visible; alongside it were two wooden poles.

"Well I never, I wonder what's in here." With care Basil lifted the box out and placed it on the dusty floor. While Sandra untied the string, Basil pulled out the poles.

"They're funny looking oars," puzzled Mark.

"They're not oars, they're baker's paddles," gasped Lottie, "Well, I never, they must be the ones Joe used."

"And look at the length of them," squeaked Hetty, "shows how deep the oven must be."

Sandra looked up. "Now they are going to look fantastic when the wall's fully exposed because I'll be able to hang them on either side of the oven door or even along the beams."

When the knot in the string finally came undone, Sandra peeped inside the box. "Old books and newspapers. How fascinating."

"Like a time capsule," Hetty knelt beside Sandra as she pulled out a 1958 copy of the Radio Times. Digging down further she found a Woman's Own magazine from the same year.

"Looks like the old oven was bricked up in 1958 then," reasoned Lottie.

"Hmm, it does, which is the same year that Eve left home with a young Norman," Hetty wondered if that fact was of any significance.

Lottie flicked through the yellowing pages of the Radio Times. "We'll have to show Norman this lot. He'll be fascinated."

"We'll give it to him," opined Sandra, "after all it must have been put here by Joe and probably after Eve scarpered with him."

Also in the box was an old Daily Mirror newspaper from February that year telling of the fatal Munich plane crash in which the Manchester United football team known as the Busby Babes were travelling. There was also a 1950s dress and white sandals which had seen better days, an empty perfume bottle, empty food packets, jars and bottles which had once contained tea, sugar, washing powder, soap, coffee, jam, cigarettes and mustard powder. Basil looked inside the oven, "Well, I never, there's another box in here as well." He pulled it out. It contained a large white linen apron with a rip down one side, a man's shabby donkey jacket, a pair of men's slippers with worn out soles and a flat cap.

"Wonderful," Hetty picked up one of the slippers, "it takes me back to my childhood. Dad had a pair like these."

Eager to see if there was anything else, Lottie peered inside the oven, "Looks like there's some old bedding at the back. I'm sure that's an eiderdown. You don't see them nowadays."

Basil reached inside, pulled the eiderdown out and shook it. A jumble of old bones clattered onto the flagstone floor and a skull rolled across the room and stopped by Lottie's feet.

Chapter Eight

The body in the oven proved to be a mystery for the police. Forensic examination established the remains were that of a white, dark-haired female who they estimated to be in her mid-thirties when she died in the late 1950s and because of the dated items in the cardboard boxes it was considered unlikely that she had died before February 1958 and although it was impossible to give the exact date, it was possible to say at what time she had died due to the broken face of a watch she had worn on her right wrist; it had stopped at one o'clock but whether that was am or pm was anyone's guess. Furthermore, because of wedding and engagement rings on the skeletal finger of her left hand they knew that she was married and the remains of the clothing she had worn indicated she was relatively well off. With the estimated knowledge of the year and details gathered, the police checked records for the nineteen fifties to see if any married woman was reported missing in and around Pentrillick but they drew a blank. They then extended their search nationwide but again to no avail and even before Forensics began their examination the police ruled out it being the remains of Eve Williams because they had visited Norman at his Dawlish home where he had produced her death certificate. Furthermore he agreed to a DNA test to see if said woman was related to him and the result was negative.

Inside the Old Bakehouse, work in the kitchen had been brought to a standstill while the police carried out various tests;

Bill was also denied access to the outhouse and so the renovation work was confined to the upstairs rooms. Consequently, by the end of the week all the bedrooms were decorated and ready for new carpets which had been chosen and were due to be fitted the following week when the police had finished their investigation. Likewise, the bathroom was also finished and the new white suite gleamed in the ceiling's spotlights. The radiators and pipework were in place ready for the engineer to install the new boiler.

On Monday, the TV film crew who had earlier filmed regarding the contents of old Joe's will, returned to the village to get the latest news and do a piece about the discovery of the body in the oven; Bill and Sandra were briefly interviewed. Off camera they were asked if they felt uncomfortable knowing a murder had been committed in their new home. Bill wisely replied that if the truth be known most houses built more than a century ago probably held dark secrets and every old home would have witnessed death at some stage. Besides, he added there was no evidence to say that the person buried in the oven had actually died in the Old Bakehouse as she could easily have been murdered elsewhere. Likewise there was no proof that it was Joe the baker who had taken her life.

"That's stretching the truth a bit," Sandra chided her husband as the film crew packed up their equipment, "after all most people think the deceased will prove to be one of the women with whom Joe had a dalliance and that seems a pretty good motive to me."

"Pure speculation, and I don't see how you can say he had a motive, after all his wife had cleared off and left him so he was foot loose and fancy free. As far as I can see there's no motive for him to kill anyone, male or female. I mean as a single man, he'd have been perfectly entitled to have a fling with whomsoever he wanted." Bill had found himself frequently defending Joe since the discovery of the body although he didn't really know why.

"Ah, but had Eve already left him when it happened? It looks to me very much as though she was still around judging by some of the things found in the oven. So I reckon she left just after it was bricked up. Poor woman probably even went because she knew what he'd done."

Bill looked smug. "In which case she'd be as guilty as Joe. Withholding information from the police is a criminal offence."

"And who can blame her for keeping quiet. I expect the poor woman was scared stiff."

"Rubbish. Anyway, why would Joe have murdered one of his lady friends in the first place? If she was one of his lady friends, that is. I mean at the moment we've no idea who she is or should I say was."

"Well at a guess I'd say the reason was because he wanted to end the affair with whoever she was. She didn't and so threatened to tell Eve. Something like that."

"Again that's pure speculation, Sandra. Besides, I reckon Eve had already gone."

"So you've said," Sandra angrily folded her arms. "So if it wasn't Joe who killed her, who was it, clever clogs?"

Bill shrugged his shoulders. "No idea. Could have been the builder, someone who worked here, anyone really."

"Humph! You're so obstinate, William. It was clearly Joe. He had an affair and his ladylove threatened to tell Eve, either because he wanted to end the affair or because he wouldn't end his marriage and marry her. Whichever it was he bumped her off. End of."

"Ah, but I've just remembered. She was married anyway so she wasn't in a position to marry anyone, was she?" Bill was triumphant.

"She could have been divorced," snapped Sandra, "or even a widow. Lots of women lost their husbands during the war."

Bill laughed. "You look really cute when you're angry. Anyway, let's not fall out over it as I'm sure we'll know something soon. You never know, Mum and Auntie Het might get on the case and find out the exact date on which the oven was bricked up and even when Eve left with Norman. If so that'll settle the argument as to whether or not Eve was around when it happened."

"You don't really believe that surely," scoffed Sandra, "I mean how could your mum and Het find out, it was sixty years ago for goodness sake."

"I haven't the foggiest idea but if they do decide to look into it I'm sure they'll find something out simply because that's the way they are."

"Hmm, well time will tell."

"Yes, it will."

Sandra smiled. "Do I really look cute when I'm angry?"

A week later, the police informed Bill and Sandra that they no longer needed access to the baking room and therefore they were free to continue with the renovation work. And so while a wood burning stove was being fitted in the sitting room, Basil and Mark continued to expose the chimney breast wall in the baking room and the heating engineer fitted the boiler in the back porch. Hetty, feeling inquisitive, volunteered to sort through the boxes of odds and ends from the cupboard beneath the stairs. Bill, meanwhile, with a day off work resumed tidying the outhouse, the girls were at school, Zac was working in the Crown and Anchor and in the sitting room Sandra and Lottie each painted the inside frames of the two front windows.

Amongst the clutter in the cupboard beneath the stairs, Hetty found a large shoebox. She removed the lid and saw it contained old receipts. Hoping amongst them she might find something alluding to the stone oven, she sat down on the bottom tread of the staircase and shuffled through the contents. To her delight she found an invoice issued by a Charlie Pascoe in February 1958 for bricking up the oven and rendering the wall. The invoice was marked paid. Delighted with her find she took it into the living room and showed it to Sandra and Lottie.

"Well, I'll be damned," laughed Sandra, as she looked at the small sheet of paper, "Bill said you'd most likely find the date when the oven was bricked up and you have."

"Did he?" Hetty was chuffed, "He usually mocks our hard work."

"Yes, he did. Now if you can find out when Eve left Joe that'll settle a little disagreement we had the other day."

"Oh, that one's easy," declared Hetty, "Eve left the village with Norman in January 1958."

"What!"

"Yes, she left a few days after her sister Alice's eighteenth birthday. It was Alice who told us when we went to see her a little while ago." Lottie carefully placed her paintbrush on top of the tin so that she could look at the invoice.

"Humph, looks like I shall have to eat humble pie then." Sandra did not look happy.

"I often have to do that," conceded Hetty, "and it's not too bad."

Lottie read the invoice. "Charlie Pascoe, I wonder if he's still around. What do you two think?"

Sandra smiled. "I doubt it, not after sixty years but then what do I know?"

"No, I suppose that is asking a bit much."

Hetty was more positive. "Depends how old he was when he did the job. I mean, if he was thirty or less then he could still be around."

Lottie glanced back at the invoice. "It says his address is 4, Main Street so we could pop along there and ask around. Someone might know something about him."

"I suppose it's worth a try," agreed Sandra, not looking forward to telling Bill of his aunt's discovery, "but despite what you say, Auntie Het, as far as I'm concerned the fact he'd have to be well over eighty means the chances of finding him are nil."

"Well, we'll go anyway," said Lottie, "it'll be nice to get away from the smell of paint."

Sandra peeled off her rubber gloves. "You must have lunch before you go. I've ordered pizzas for everyone and they should be delivered anytime now."

"Better hurry up and get this window finished then. I'm on the last bit." Lottie picked up her paintbrush.

Sandra looked smug. "I've finished mine."

"I must admit they've come up really well," said Hetty, admiring the windows, "and look as good as new."

Sandra nodded. "Yes, they have thank goodness as it'd cost a few bob to replace them like for like."

"Like for like," repeated Hetty, "What do you mean?"

"The house is Grade Two listed. At least the front of it is so we can't change the door and windows unless they're exactly the same, meaning like for like."

Hetty tutted. "I didn't know that. Oh dear, so no UPVC double glazing then."

Sandra shook her head. "Absolutely not and that hideous front door has to stay as well."

"Oh, I think it's rather nice," enthused Hetty, "and I'm sure after it's had a lick of paint it'll look splendid."

"You do? Then you can rub it down and paint it," laughed Sandra.

"I will," Hetty was always up for a challenge, "and I think you'll be amazed by the outcome."

Bill walked in and caught the end of the conversation. "Talking of paint, I've got to the old trunk at last. Come and see."

The three ladies followed Bill to the outhouse where he lifted the lid of the trunk. It was full of old paints, picture frames, brushes, old cloths and an easel along with several paintings.

Bill lifted out one of small birds feeding on a bird table; it was signed Joe Williams.

Lottie was impressed. "So it looks as though painting was his hobby and very good he was too."

"What are the rest of?" Hetty asked.

"From what I can see most are birds," Bill lifted out an oil painting of seagulls on a beach and another of a robin resting on the handle of a garden spade with a sprig of mistletoe in its beak.

Sandra, keen to extract one from the old trunk herself, clasped the edge of a dark wooden frame. It came out back-to-front. When she turned it, she gasped. The picture was of a raven on a rooftop encircled by a bright full moon.

To the surprise of the sisters when they knocked on the door of number 4 Main Street later in the afternoon, it was answered by Natalie Burleigh, a young woman who for a time with her husband Luke had rented a cottage a few doors away from Primrose Cottage along Blackberry Way.

"Oh, we didn't realise you lived here," Hetty felt rather foolish, "I mean, we knew you lived along here somewhere but not which house."

Natalie looked bewildered.

Lottie attempted to defuse the confusion. "We're trying to track down someone who lived here sixty years ago but of course it was long before you came to the village so I don't suppose you'll know anything of him."

"Oh, oh, I see." It was clear by the expression on Natalie's face that she didn't.

"It's to do with the body in the oven," blurted Hetty.

Natalie's face lit up. "Really! Would you like to come in for a coffee then? Please say you will because I'd love to hear the latest news. It's the talk of the village."

"Yes, coffee would be very nice, thank you." Hetty stepped over the threshold and Lottie followed.

"So, out of curiosity who are you looking for?" Natalie asked when they were all seated in the sitting room.

"A chap called Charlie Pascoe. He used to be a builder who lived in this house and we have every reason to believe that he was the chap who bricked up the old oven." Hetty pulled the builder's invoice from her pocket.

As Natalie took the small sheet of paper and read it, she frowned. "How old do you think this Charlie Pascoe would be now?"

Hetty shrugged her shoulders. "Well, according to this invoice, the oven was bricked up in February 1958 so he must have been twenty plus then in which case he's got to be in his eighties now if he's still alive."

"Really, now that is interesting." Natalie folded the invoice and passed it back to Hetty.

Lottie leaned forwards in her chair. "Do you mean you know something about him then?"

Natalie nodded. "Maybe. You see up at the care home we have an old chap called Charlie Pascoe and he's well into his eighties. In fact he's eighty five. It was his birthday last week. I don't know whether or not he ever lived here though but if he did and he's the right Charlie it'll be fascinating to ask him about it."

Hetty gasped. "We forgot you worked up at the care home. Surely it's got to be him."

"Is your Charlie from the village?" Lottie eagerly asked.

"Yes, definitely because he often talks about when he was a boy and how he went to the village school. Having said that, talk of yesteryear is when he's having a good day. On bad days he can't even remember his own name."

"Do you think we could visit him?" Hetty crossed her fingers.

"Of course. You'd be welcome any time."

"Excellent, we'll pop along and see him sometime this week depending on when and if we're needed to help out at the Old Bakehouse. Although there's not much more we can do now. I've volunteered to paint the front door but that can be done anytime."

Lottie laughed. "I think you'll find a dry day might be useful and this time of the year they're few and far between."

"True but it won't take long and I've got to rub it down first anyway."

"So is there any news as to who the body in the oven might have been?" Natalie asked, "Someone told me it was female but I've heard no more than that."

"Yes, the poor soul was a married, dark haired female and they think the possible cause of death was strangulation," said Hetty.

"And it's reckoned she would have been in her mid-thirties when she died," Lottie added. "The police have checked records to see if any female of that age was reported missing in 1958 but I don't think they've had any luck."

Hetty nodded. "And that's where Charlie Pascoe comes in. We're hoping he might know something. The invoice might even jog his memory."

"How exciting," giggled Natalie.

Lottie scowled. "I've just had a thought, Het. Do you think we ought to tell the police about the invoice and the fact the chap who bricked up the oven might still be around?"

"Hmm, not sure about that. I think it might be best if we speak to Charlie first and see what he has to say. After all there's always the chance he might not be the right Charlie anyway."

"But surely not to do so is withholding vital evidence, information or whatever they call it."

"Yes, I agree and if the crime had been committed recently then it would be more pressing but after all this time I can't see anyone doing a runner especially as the most likely culprit is old Joe Williams who of course is dead."

"Yes, I suppose you're right." Lottie spoke without conviction.

"Don't look so glum. We'll speak to Charlie. If he's the right chap and he remembers bricking up the oven, then we'll tell that nice detective inspector chappie who called the other day."

"Detective Inspector Fox."

"Yes, that's the one."

Chapter Nine

The following day, Hetty and Lottie left Primrose Cottage and walked to the care home situated up a narrow lane behind the village school. It was a two storey building just over fifty years old and with lots of windows on the southern side. The grounds were nicely laid out and although not many flowers were in bloom it was obvious the garden would be a picture in the summer.

"Lovely and bright," whispered Hetty, as they stepped inside having informed the person who answered the door wearing a name badge who they wished to see.

"Are you relatives of Mr Pascoe?" they were asked as the door was closed and then locked.

"No, um, err, Lynn," said Hetty, focussing on the name badge. Before she had a chance to say more, Natalie Burleigh appeared in the hallway.

"Oh, hello. Have you come to see Charlie?"

"I take it you know these ladies," Lynn spoke to Natalie.

"Yes, I've known them ever since Luke and I moved to Pentrillick. We're old friends. Isn't that so, Hetty and Lottie?"

The sisters nodded.

"That's okay then. I'll leave you to it."

"Security's a bit tight here," commented Lottie, "I'm pleased to see it though. It wouldn't do to have any Tom, Dick or Harry wandering around poking through the residents' possessions."

Natalie led the sisters into the day room with panoramic views of the sea where an elderly gentleman sat by a window reading a paperback book with a garish front cover.

Natalie gently touched his arm. "Charlie, you have visitors."

He looked up and frowned. "Hello, ladies. Do I know you?"

Lottie shook her head. "No, but we believe you might be the builder who once upon a time worked on a house in the village which my son and his family have just bought."

Charlie laughed. "Not come to complain about my workmanship, I hope."

"Oh, no, no, nothing like that."

"Only kidding. Sit down, ladies."

"I'll leave you now," said Natalie, "but tell one of the carers when you're ready to leave and he or she will see you out."

Hetty nodded. "Will do."

"So, what can I do for you?" Charlie asked as the sisters sat. "But before that you must tell me your names?"

"I'm Hetty."

"I'm Lottie and we're sisters. Twins in fact."

"And we've come to ask you about the Old Bakehouse," gushed Hetty, not wishing to beat about the bush. "As Lottie said, we have reason to believe you did some work there sixty years ago."

Charlie chuckled. "I did work everywhere, can you be more precise?"

"You bricked up the old oven in the baking room and then rendered the wall."

"Did I? That sounds a bit daft because Joe would've needed it to bake the bread."

Hetty sat up straight. "You remember Joe then."

"Of course I do, he was the baker. He's dead now though, isn't he? Someone told me the other day but I can't recall who." Charlie tutted. "Poor chap. I remember him crying when his wife left him. He was devastated and said he'd never marry again because if he did it'd most like end in tears. His first wife died, you see. Such a shame. Poor old Joe."

"So do you remember bricking up the oven?" Hetty asked.

"Can't say that I do."

"It was back in 1958," Lottie hoped mention of the year might help.

"1958!" he laughed, "I were only a lad then," He started to calculate the figures in his head but appeared confused.

"If you're eighty-five now you must have been born in 1933," Lottie determined.

"That's right, I was. When were you ladies born?"

"1952," said Hetty.

Charlie frowned. "What both of you?"

"Yes, we're twins."

"Oh yes, you did say," He glanced towards the window where sunlight reflected on a crystal vase containing yellow and white chrysanthemums. "Why do you want to know about the old oven?"

"No reason," Hetty suddenly felt that mention of the body might be too much for the elderly man to take in. "It's only that Lottie's son and his wife have just bought the Old Bakehouse and amongst the things we found in a box under the stairs is the invoice you issued for bricking up the oven and rendering up the wall. Look I have it here." She handed it to Charlie.

"Yes, that'd be one of mine. I didn't write it though."

"You didn't?" Hetty looked confused.

"No, that's Audrey's writing. She was my wife but she's gone now. My writing's terrible so she did all my paperwork." He handed the invoice back to Hetty, "So why did you say you wanted to know about the old oven?"

Lottie, following Hetty's train of thought regarding mention of the body being too much for Charlie to comprehend, quickly answered, "We were just wondering if you could remember what it was all like back then."

"Give me a couple of days and I'll think about it," He chuckled and tapped his head, "It'll all be up here in the old computer somewhere; I just need to flush it out."

"Of course, there's no rush," said Lottie.

"Did you know that Natalie who works here and her husband live in the house you used to live in?" Hetty hoped mention of the house might bring back memories of the past.

"Yes, she asked me where I used to live this morning when she brought me my breakfast. When I told her it was 4, Main Street she was fascinated. After she'd gone I looked out my old photo album and then when she came to collect my breakfast tray I showed her some pictures of me and Audrey in the garden there. Would you like to see them?"

"Yes, please," gushed Hetty.

Charlie reached under his chair. "Oh, bother wrong chair the album's under the one in my room."

"Never mind," smiled Lottie, "perhaps we can see them another time."

"Yes, yes, we'll do that and I'll make sure the album is in here."

After the sisters' chat with Charlie they went out into the hallway in search of someone to tell that they were leaving; ambling along the corridor they saw Natalie escorting an elderly lady with a walking frame.

"Are you off?" Natalie called.

Lottie took gloves from her pocket and put them on. "Yes, we'll come back and see Charlie again another day, if we may. He said to do so as he's got some photos of your garden to show us."

"Yes, he showed them to me this morning. I must admit it brought a lump to my throat."

Lottie smiled. "Yes, I bet it did."

"Anyway, I'm glad you're going to come back to see Charlie because our residents are always glad to have visitors."

"We look forward to it," said Hetty, "He's good company."

"Umm, did he…umm…remember doing the brickwork in the Old Bakehouse?" Natalie was careful not to mention the oven in case any of the residents heard.

Hetty shook her head. "No, but he reckons if we give him a few days it'll all come back to him. I know what he means because it's the same with me."

"And me," chuckled the lady with the walking frame, "I often struggle to remember things but when I do get my mind in the right groove it all comes back crystal clear."

"Ah, yes, now this lady is also someone you might like to meet." Natalie put her hand on the elderly lady's shoulder. "Hetty, Lottie, may I introduce you to Nellie Gibson. Nellie used to be a midwife and has lived in the village all her life."

"Really," gasped Hetty, "that's an occupation close to my heart. I used to be a midwife too you see."

Nellie's mouth formed a near-perfect O. "One day then when you've time you must come and visit me for a chat."

"Well, there's no time like the present," said Hetty, eagerly, "that's unless you're expecting another visitor."

Nellie chuckled. "No, I'm not expecting anyone before the weekend. "My son lives in Totnes, you see and so he can only get away then."

Chapter Ten

Just before dusk on Friday afternoon, a couple in their mid-seventies walked up to the reception desk in the Pentrillick Hotel to book into the room for which they had a made a reservation online."

"And may I have your names, please?" Anna, the receptionist on duty asked.

"Bridget Barnes, Mrs, but everyone calls me Biddy, and this is my husband, Geoff Barnes."

"Ah, yes, you have a double room booked and have requested a sea view." Anna took a key card from beneath the desk and handed it to Biddy, "One of our porters will see you to your room. I hope you have a pleasant stay with us." She nodded to a young man who waited across the foyer.

Biddy picked up her handbag from the desk. "Thank you, dear. I hope we do too."

"Beautiful view," said Geoff, as they stepped into their room, "May I have the side of the bed nearest the window, please, Bids?"

"Of course. I'd prefer to be near the bathroom door anyway as I'm bound to get up in the night."

Biddy sat down on the bed and removed her shoes. "The bed feels comfy so that's good."

Geoff crossed the room, opened up the window and then sat down on its cushioned seat. "Hmm, not only is this view spectacular but so is the smell of the sea air. Come and have a sniff."

Biddy joined him on the window seat and took in a deep breath. "Yes, it is lovely although a little chilly to have the window open."

"I'll shut it in a minute." He took her hand. "Anyway, we've made it, Biddy."

"Yes, we've made it and I like what I've seen so far."

"I agree. It looks a nice place. I wouldn't mind living here myself."

Biddy smiled. "So you could go fishing no doubt."

"You can read me like a book. Anyway, this trip isn't about me it's about you. So when do you want to start looking into the past?"

"I don't know. I don't even know where to start looking."

"Well, I suppose the pub would be the most logical place to ask questions."

Biddy laughed. "Trust you to think of that."

"Well, we are on a sort of holiday, aren't we?"

"Yes, you're right and I'd like to go to the pub anyway and if we don't find out anything there we can always take a walk round the churchyard because I'm sure both my biological parents will have passed away by now."

Geoff looked at his wife. "Are you going to be alright with this, Biddy? I mean, it must be hard for you."

"Yes, I'll be fine. I just wish I'd done it sooner, that's all. But it wouldn't have been fair, would it? And I didn't want to hurt Mum and Dad. I mean, they didn't need to tell me I was adopted, did they?" Biddy's shoulders slumped, "In a way it might have been better if they hadn't."

Geoff put his arm around his wife's narrow shoulders. "Maybe, but they did tell you and whatever the outcome of this, you'll always think of them as your parents."

"Yes, I shall." Biddy got up from the window seat, reached for her handbag and took out a packet of cigarettes and a lighter.

"I won't be many minutes, Geoff, and then when I get back I'll unpack our stuff."

"I wish you'd give up smoking. You were coughing in your sleep last night."

"Was I?"

"Yes."

"Well I'll give up in January. It's not far away now and it can be my New Year's resolution."

Geoff shook his head in dismay. "You say that every year."

"But this time I promise I'll stick to it." She walked towards the door.

"Okay, but before you go out remind me: what are the names of your birth parents again? I remember your mother was Cicely but have forgotten your father's name."

Biddy opened the door. "Joseph Percival Williams was my father and according to my birth certificate he was a baker."

Meanwhile, further down the road on an allotted parking space beside Sea View Cottage, a blue Renault car pulled up and from it stepped two women, who judging by their features were clearly mother and daughter. From the boot of the car they took two suitcases; the name label on one was Irene Hewitt and the other Martha Hewitt. With cases in hand they wheeled them round to the back of the cottage where they found a key to the house beneath a large terracotta pot containing winter flowering pansies.

"Well, we're here," said the younger of the two women, "so where shall we start, Mum?"

Irene sighed. "Start what, Martha? Do you mean with settling in?"

"Well, no I was thinking more on the lines of tracing your ancestors."

Irene laughed. "Well, I suppose Willow House is as good a place as any, after all that's where we used to live. Not that the house will be able to tell us anything but at least it might jog my memory back into the right groove. Anyway, before we do anything I'd like to get my things unpacked and make myself at home."

Martha picked up both suitcases and walked towards the stairs. "Of course, come on then, let's choose our rooms. I believe there are four so we'll be spoiled for choice."

After their things were unpacked they returned downstairs.

"Would you like a cup of tea?" Martha asked, as she took a container of milk from a carrier bag.

"Yes, please. Then after that and I've had a little rest we'll take a walk through the village although we won't see much now it's dark. I must admit I'm looking forward to seeing the old place again."

"Me too. Not that I've ever seen it before."

However, after the tea Irene fell asleep on the couch and didn't wake until after eight when she found her daughter watching the news channel on the television and a fire burning in the grate. She sat up promptly. "Oh, Martha, why didn't you wake me, dear?"

"Because I considered the sleep would do you good and we're here for a week anyway so there's no rush." Martha refrained from telling her mother that she looked tired and older than her seventy years.

"And you've lit a fire. Where did you find the logs?"

"In a shed out the back. I know the heating's on but I lit the fire because it's nice to look at. Anyway, I don't know about you, Mum, but I'm feeling a bit peckish so after we've taken a walk through the village I suggest we pop into a pub, assuming there is one here of course."

"Yes, there's a pub, at least there was when I was a girl and if I remember correctly it's called the Crown and Anchor." She stood up. "I think I'll pop upstairs and change first though. I feel quite chilly having had a nap and so need to put on something warmer."

As they left Sea View Cottage and stepped into the main street, Irene glanced back at the Old Bakehouse just visible further along the road but she said nothing to her daughter.

"So whereabouts is Willow House?" Martha asked.

"St Mary's Avenue but we'll not bother to go up there tonight since it's dark: we'll leave it until tomorrow."

"Okay, so has the village changed much?" Martha was aware that her mother's head was turning back and forth as she tried to take in both sides of the road.

"No more than you'd expect after sixty years."

When they arrived at the Crown and Anchor they found it to be very busy.

"Good heavens," laughed Martha, as they stepped inside, "I should have thought the place would be quiet on a weekday night in November."

"Me likewise. Perhaps there's something on. A party maybe."

"I don't think so because no-one is wearing party clothes."

Martha went to the bar to buy drinks, and Irene, realising all the tables were taken warmed her hands by the log fire. As Martha returned and handed her mother a glass of white wine, Irene caught the eye of a lady sitting with two other women.

"There's room for two more on this table," said Hetty, "that's if you don't mind sharing."

"Are you sure?" Irene asked.

"Of course."

"Then yes please. I must admit I don't like standing, especially with a drink in one hand and my bag in the other."

Hetty, Lottie and their friend Debbie moved around the table to make room.

"It's busy in here tonight," said Martha, wondering if the three ladies might be able to say why.

"Yes, we've only just got here and if it wasn't for the fact some people left as we arrived we'd be standing up too."

"So why is it so busy?" Irene asked, "Is there something on?"

"Several people are strangers so they could well be treasure hunters," laughed Debbie.

"And the locals in here are keen to hear the latest gossip," Hetty added, "and that includes us."

Irene and Martha were clearly nonplussed.

"I take it you're not from around here then," Lottie noted their confused expressions.

"No, no, we're from Bath."

"Ah, Somerset," said Debbie, "beautiful county."

"On holiday?" Hetty asked.

"Well, no not really," Irene sipped her wine, "We're here to see if I can find out what happened to my mother who reputedly left my father many years ago for another man. I was ten years old when she left and then two months later my father and I moved away to Portsmouth. I've not really thought much about it over the years but when my best friend died last month it got me thinking of the past and I wanted to see if I could find out what happened to Mother. Pentrillick seemed the obvious place to start."

"Oh, I am sorry, about your friend that is," commiserated Lottie.

"Thank you. I'm Irene, by the way, and this young lady is my daughter, Martha."

"Not so young, Mother, I'm thirty-eight now."

Hetty laughed. "That's young to us, Martha. Anyway, pleased to meet you both. I'm Hetty and this is my twin sister, Lottie and the dear lady next to me is our very good friend, Debbie."

They all shook hands.

"So, what can you tell us about your mother?" Lottie asked, "We might be able to help although I doubt it as we're all relatively new to the area ourselves."

Irene smiled. "I can't really tell you a great deal but I do know that she was called Geraldine and was born in 1922. Her married name was Glover; her maiden name was Trelease. She was beautiful and sadly she and my father seemed to argue a lot. He always insisted she was a flighty piece and was unfaithful to him. At one time he even accused her of having an affair with the baker. When she went I recall him saying good riddance and he didn't seem to care. In fact in later years he began to doubt that I was his daughter and so we both took DNA tests. Sadly he was right but I still regarded him as my father although our relationship after that was never the same again. Not until he died, that is. Just before his death he told me he was sorry and said that perhaps it was his fault that my mother had strayed into the arms of another and deprived me of her love and friendship."

"That's really sad," sympathised Debbie, "it must have been very hard for you."

Irene nodded. "It was but it's history now and I've long since moved on."

"So when did your mother leave the village?" Hetty asked.

"When I was ten years old so that would have been in 1958 and I remember the month, it was February. It was weird, she just went off without taking any of her possessions, not even her treasured Buddy Holly records. After that we never heard from her again."

Hetty choked on her wine.

"Are you all right?" Irene patted her back.

Hetty looked at her sister and then at Debbie.

"February 1958 and you say you never heard from your mother again after she left?" Lottie felt her cheeks burning.

Irene shook her head. "No, which in retrospect seems heartless, don't you think? I mean, you'd have thought that she'd have sent me birthday and Christmas cards. She wouldn't have needed to say where she was or who she was with but just let us know that she was alive, well and happy."

Martha looked across the crowded bar. "You never did explain to us what you meant by the people here being treasure hunters."

The jaws of the three ladies dropped.

"I think I need another drink. A large one," gulped Hetty, rising, "Anyone else for a refill?"

Lottie and Debbie held up their quickly drained glasses.

"We're fine," smiled Irene.

"Okay, I'll be back as soon as I can and then between us we'll fill you in with the village's latest."

Chapter Eleven

Over the weekend several more people descended on Pentrillick keen to find out more about Joe on the off chance they might be able to put in a claim. Amongst them were Jim Bray and his mother, Pamela who had booked into Tuzzy-Muzzy, the first house along Blackberry Way where the owners offered bed and breakfast.

"I was chatting to a couple just now who are staying next door in the guest house," said Debbie, as she took off her coat and hung it on the pegs in the hallway of Primrose Cottage on Monday morning, "They're mother and son and they got here yesterday afternoon. Pamela, the mother, is convinced Joe is the boy's father. Well, I say boy but he's actually a man and a tall one at that like his mother. She towered over me."

"Not another," chuckled Hetty, as she closed the front door and escorted Debbie into the sitting room, "Where are they from?"

"Bodmin apparently."

"I heard that," Lottie looked up from her knitting where she sat in a fireside chair, "Do you think they're genuine or just here on the off-chance?"

Debbie sat down at the table. "No idea, but Jim, the son, was born in 1971 and Pamela, his mum, says she's often wondered what happened to the boy's father who was definitely called Joe."

Hetty tutted. "Looks like Pentrillick was a den of vice back when old Joe was alive."

"It certainly does," agreed Debbie. "So have you fathomed out what happened at the bakery back in 1958? Because I haven't."

"Not really," Hetty sat down opposite their guest, "I mean the obvious surmise is that Joe killed Geraldine Glover and hid her body in the oven. We know she had an affair with him because he was Irene's father…"

"…Ah, but was he, Het?" Lottie interrupted, "at present we only suspect he is because Irene said her father reckoned she was the daughter of a baker."

"True but for the sake of argument let's assume for now that Joe was her father and then we can move on and explore possible reasons as to why Joe might have killed her."

Lottie put down her knitting and joined her sister and Debbie at the table. "Well, we'll soon know one way or another because Irene's going to have another DNA test done. As for a reason for killing her, I've no idea what that might have been."

"Me neither but we should be able to come up with at least one motive," reasoned Hetty, "Come on, ladies, put your thinking caps on and use your imaginations."

All three sat quietly for a whole minute.

"I suppose it's possible that Geraldine wanted to marry Joe and demanded that he divorced Eve to enable them to do so and Joe said no," suggested Debbie, "Geraldine might then have threatened to tell Eve and so Joe killed her to shut her up."

"That was one of Sandra's theories before we knew who the body was," sighed Lottie, "but it wouldn't have been that simple, would it? Remember Geraldine was married too and so not free to marry either."

Hetty smiled. "What's more it can't be the answer because by February when the murder took place Eve had already gone and taken young Norman with her so she wouldn't have been around for Geraldine to tell anyway."

Debbie groaned. "Of course, I'd forgotten that."

"Maybe Geraldine's husband killed her then," reasoned Lottie, "after all Irene told us that her father, or the man she assumed was her father until both took DNA tests which proved otherwise, wasn't a bit bothered by his wife's disappearance and even said good riddance. What's more, he and Geraldine argued a lot so they clearly didn't get on."

Debbie nodded. "Yes, he'd certainly have a good motive and he obviously didn't even report her as missing."

"But how could he have put her body in the oven?" Hetty asked.

Lottie's shoulders slumped. "I don't know and it's not possible to put ourselves in their shoes because we don't know who had access to the house and stuff like that. It'd help if Charlie could remember the day he bricked it up but sadly he can't. Not at the moment anyway."

"I suppose someone could have broken into the Old Bakehouse while Joe was at work," reasoned Debbie, "because we know he closed up the business when Eve left and if that was in the January then by February he could well have been working at Pentrillick House."

Hetty laughed. "Oh, Debbie that conjures up such a silly picture. Can you really imagine that someone would break in after carrying a body through the streets and then shove it in the back of the oven?"

Lottie gasped. "Actually, I can. I mean, if the business was closed and it was common knowledge that the oven was to be bricked up, then someone might have seen it as the perfect hiding place especially if they knew about the boxes of memorabilia to be hidden because they would provide the perfect cover. And the body wouldn't need to be carried; it could have been dropped off by a vehicle of some sort. It could even have been a delivery man with a van: the postman, milkman, butcher or someone like that. Lots of businesses did deliveries back in the fifties."

Debbie nodded. "Absolutely and the chances are that Charlie bricked it up while Joe was at work and so either Joe would have left a key somewhere for Charlie to get in or maybe even left the place unlocked. After all people were much more trusting back in the fifties: my mum often went out without locking up and thought nothing of it."

Hetty leaned back in her chair. "Hmm, I think you might be onto something there. So now we must regard anyone who we think might have had a motive as a definite suspect."

"Trouble is after sixty years they'll most likely all be dead," reasoned Lottie.

Hetty nodded. "Yes, but it'll still be a nice challenge for us to work out who did it and I'm sure the ever increasing number of Joe's offspring would like to see his name cleared too."

During the winter months, Monday evening was pool night and the Crown and Anchor team played either at home or away. This Monday they were at home for a match against the Rose and Crown from Polquillick, a picturesque fishing village on the Lizard peninsula. Team captain Kyle was confident they would do well. They had a strong team and were pleased to welcome a new member, Zac, who had been eager to join ever since he had moved to the village. To make sure he was able to play consistently, Ashley the landlord agreed that Monday must always be one of the days when Zac didn't work behind the bar.

Pool night was always a good night at the Crown and Anchor when the team were home for they had a small following of youngsters; amongst them were newcomers, Vicki and Kate.

"Why aren't there any girls on the team?" Vicki asked as Kyle and the team practised before the arrival of their opponents.

"Girls would be most welcome if they could play," said Kyle, "but most umm…well…aren't competitive enough."

"Which is Kyle's diplomatic way of saying girls are rubbish," laughed Zac.

"Humph!" Vicki wanted to argue but she knew neither she nor Kate played well and neither did Zac's girlfriend, Emma.

"Practice makes perfect," advised Luke Burleigh, "because I have to admit I wasn't much cop when Nat and I first moved here but now I'm quite happy to take on anyone."

"What even Ronnie O'Sullivan?" Vicki teased.

"He's plays snooker, you muppet," tutted Zac.

Vicki scowled. "Same thing surely."

All the team members laughed.

"How can we get to be better than them?" Vicki whispered behind her hand to Kate.

"We can't," giggled Kate, "remember we tried our hand at the sports club in Kettering and when we played each other the match went on for ever."

"Hmm, you're right, in which case we must try and find a female who can play well and then she can teach us."

On Tuesday evening Lottie, Hetty and Debbie went to play bingo in the village hall and afterwards they popped into the Crown and Anchor to catch up with the latest gossip. As Debbie waited at the bar to buy drinks she saw Geoff Barnes was all alone. "No Biddy tonight?"

Geoff tutted. "Yes, she's here and gone out for a fag."

"Oh, I see. I didn't realise she smoked."

"She has smoked since she was fourteen and every year says she'll give up but I doubt she ever will. I hoped the smoking ban, meaning she would have to go outside, might push her towards kicking the habit but it seems to have made very little difference."

Debbie ordered three glasses of wine. "You both have my sympathy, Geoff. I was a smoker too until I gave up in 2001. Gideon nagged me for years and he won in the end."

"Gideon?"

"My husband."

"I see."

With drinks in hand, Debbie returned to Lottie and Hetty and as they chatted, a young man walked into the bar. Several local people greeted him; so saw Hetty who watched from the corner of her eye. Judging by the bonhomie she concluded that he must be from the area. However, never having seen him before she was curious to ascertain who he was and so mentioned it to Lottie and Debbie; both agreed they had never seen him before either. Hetty who was a stranger to patience, quickly drained her glass.

"Drink up, ladies. I'm going up for refills so that I can ask Tess."

"But it's my round now," Lottie placed her empty glass on the table.

"You go and ask then."

"What! Good heavens, no. I don't want Tess to think I'm nosy." Lottie quickly grabbed her handbag and from her purse pulled a twenty pound note. "You go for me, Het. She knows you're nosy."

"Humph!" Hetty took the proffered money along with the three empty glasses and went to the bar.

"Well?" Lottie asked when she returned.

"His name is Ding Dong Bell." Hetty carefully put down the three refills.

Lottie rubbed her ears convinced she had heard wrong.

"His name is what?" Debbie laughed.

"Ding Dong Bell." Hetty sat down, took Lottie's change from her pocket and laid it on the table. "It's not his real name of course. His real name is Douglas."

"So why did you say he was Ding Dong Bell?" Lottie picked up her change.

"Because his name is Douglas Bell, well actually Douglas Daniel Bell and would you believe he likes ringing church bells?"

Lottie and Debbie both looked nonplussed.

"You're pulling our legs," Lottie frowned.

"I'm not honestly. You go and ask Tess."

Eventually Hetty told Lottie and Debbie what she had learned. "Douglas has been known as Ding Dong ever since he'd started secondary school when some bright spark back then spotted D. D. Bell on his satchel. You can imagine that amusing school boys, can't you? And the fact that he liked ringing bells was purely coincidental but now that he's back in the village he'll no doubt help with the bell ringing as he did before he went away."

"Where's he been then?" Lottie asked.

"Not sure but Tess said he'd been abroad for three years teaching young children along with missionary workers or something like that. He's twenty four by the way in case you were wondering."

"So where's he living now he's back?" Debbie asked.

"With his parents in Hawthorn Road. He's a qualified teacher apparently and now he's back he'll be teaching at the village school but not until after the Christmas holidays when a Mr Brooks, who I'm told currently teaches the older children, retires.

"Well, if he likes to ring the bells we'll probably see him in church," reasoned Lottie, "we could certainly do with a few fresh faces although there are more now than there were before Vicar Sam arrived in the parish."

Shortly after a couple emerged from the dining room; Debbie nodded in their direction and whispered, "Ah, look over there, that's the mother and son from Bodmin I was telling you about. The ones staying at Tuzzy-Muzzy."

"Hetty gasped. "Blimey I see what you mean, she is tall. Must nearly be a six footer. I wouldn't want to pick a fight with her."

"Me neither," chuckled Lottie, "What's more, I can't see any likeness there between the young chap she's with and the pictures I've seen of Joe, so I reckon they're here on a wild goose chase."

Debbie nodded. "I thought the same thing when I met them yesterday. Having said that he looks a bit like his mother so could still be one of Joe's offspring."

When mother and son had drinks in hand they crossed to the table next to the ladies. As Jim sat, his jacket caught the buckle on Hetty's handbag and knocked in onto the floor. "Oh, no, sorry guys," He hastily picked the bag up.

"No problem." Hetty smiled sweetly, delighted to have reason to speak to the pair, "A little bird told me that you think you might be one of Joe's offspring."

"How on earth do you know that?" He then noticed Debbie. "Ah, you're the lady we saw yesterday morning."

Debbie nodded. "That's right and these two ladies," she pointed to Hetty and Lottie, "live next door to the guest house where you're staying."

They each introduced themselves.

"Cool," Jim was keen to make friends, "Can I get you guys a drink?"

"Not for me," replied Hetty. Debbie and Lottie agreed with nods of their heads.

"So have you had your DNA taken yet?" Debbie asked.

"Yep, done this afternoon. Just waiting for the results now," Jim downed half of his pint in one go.

"They'll be positive." Pamela was emphatic.

Jim nodded. "Yeah, so you keep saying, Mum."

"Would it be indelicate to ask why you think Joe is your father?" Hetty asked.

Jim shrugged his shoulders. "You'd have to ask Mum that. I never knew the guy."

Pamela put down her glass. "I met Joe many years ago at a night club in Penzance. He told me he lived in Pentrillick and that made a bond between us because at the time I was working at the care home here. We went out for a couple of months and I really liked him but I never saw where he lived because when we went out it was in Penzance where I lived and so we always went back to my place."

"You worked in the care home here," Lottie interrupted, "it must have been quite new then."

"Yes, it was built in 1965 and I worked there from day one but only for a few years."

Lottie tutted. "I see. Sorry I interrupted, Pamela, please continue."

"Well, one day when I was at work someone told me that Joe had a wife who had left him back in the late fifties and so strictly speaking he was still married. As far as I was concerned that was it so I ended the relationship the next time I saw him, simple as that. I mean, I was looking for a husband and a bit of security but he wasn't free to marry so it was a no brainer. Seven months later Jim was born and by then I'd met someone else. We married, moved to Bodmin and Alan brought Jim up as though he was his own but Jim knew that Alan wasn't his real dad from a very early age." Pamela picked up her glass and took a large gulp of vodka and Coke, "Mind you, I'm none too happy to learn that Joe killed someone so in a way I wouldn't be too upset if the DNA results are negative but I'm one hundred percent sure that won't be the case." She looked at her son, "Anyway, Jim's more like me than Joe in temperament and in looks and I'm sure there's not a bad streak in him. As for the money, I feel we're entitled to a share as much as anyone else including the legitimate son I've heard about." She laughed, "Alan, my late husband, used to call Jim, Lucky Jim, so let's hope on this occasion he's right."

"Late husband," repeated Lottie.

"Yes, sadly Alan passed away a year ago. He had a heart attack and died in the ambulance. Poor soul, I really miss him."

The next morning, Hetty and Lottie drove down to the Old Bakehouse with Sandra to be there for when the two carpet fitters arrived to carpet out the four bedrooms. While the two men set about their work, Hetty took a sheet of sand paper and a cushion out to the front of the house and began to rub down the paintwork on the old door. After an hour of excessive use of elbow grease its appearance was much improved.

"What colour do you want it painted?" Hetty asked when Sandra handed her a mug of tea.

Sandra shrugged her shoulders. "I don't really mind but since you like the door you must choose."

"In which case it has to be white or maybe yellow. Oh yes, definitely yellow, daffodil yellow because it's such a happy colour."

"Hmm, sounds good. I'll get Bill to pick up a tin of paint then when he finishes work tomorrow." Sandra forced a smile as she deviously planned that Bill would get a light cream shade rather than yellow accidently on purpose.

"No need, we have a tin of yellow gloss paint in our garage left over from when I painted some flower pots and there's more than enough left to do this. Meanwhile I'll put some undercoat on because there's still some left from when you and Lottie did the windows." Hetty stood up and took a sip of tea. "It'll look smashing when it's done and be the talk of the village."

Sandra winced as she visualised the bright yellow paint and then a thought occurred to her. "You know, it's only just struck me but this will be the very door that Geraldine Glover walked through back in February 1958 little knowing that she'd never see the light of day again."

Hetty shuddered. "That's a very morbid thought but I doubt it's the same door. This looks very nineteen sixties to me. In fact Joe probably had it changed a few years after he closed the shop."

"True but it's still the same threshold," Sandra stepped out onto the pavement and looked back at the house. "It's such a shame that inanimate objects can't talk, don't you think? Because if they could what a tale they'd have to tell."

For a few minutes no traffic passed by and Hetty was able to imagine the shop in days-gone-by. With eyes closed she visualised ladies in elegant long dresses crossing the threshold to be greeted by Joe's ancestors. She could almost smell the bread, hear the sound of horses trotting by and the laughter of children playing in the street. The spell was broken when Lottie popped her head round the door. "They've finished carpeting two of the bedrooms already. Come and see."

The following evening after dark, Douglas Bell walked down to the village to meet other bell ringers for a quick practice before choir members arrived for their weekly run through of the following Sunday's hymns. As he walked beneath the lich gate and onto the gravel path he spotted a lone figure wearing dark coloured clothes and a baseball cap in the churchyard; the figure was crouched and appeared to be hiding behind an old crooked tombstone. It was not possible to identify said person because he was only just visible in the shadow of the street lamp and Douglas deemed it was unlikely he would know him anyway.

Chuckling to himself he continued along the path and entered the church where he was greeted by old friends delighted to see him back.

Chapter Twelve

On Saturday evening, two more people turned up in search of their inheritance. It was Sid the plumber who got to meet them first; as he stood at the bar in the Crown and Anchor enjoying a pint one of the two latest arrivals spoke to him, "Do you know anything about the bloke who died recently and is now looking for his long lost sons and daughters?"

Sid chuckled. "I don't think Joe's looking for anyone now he's six feet under but if you mean the executors of his will then yes, I know a bit about it."

"Care to fill us in?"

"Yes, of course, I'll be glad to oblige," he held out his hand, "I'm Sid by the way, and I'm a plumber."

"Oh, really now that's interesting because we're tradesmen too. General builders in fact though stonework's our speciality and we have our own business."

"Self-employed then. That's the way forward."

"Yes, I'd hate to work for someone although we both did for a while when we started out and had to learn the ropes."

"So do you have names?"

The taller of the two men laughed. "Yes, sorry. I'm Harry and this is my brother Larry. We're twins, not that we look anything like each other."

Sid smiled. "Harry and Larry. Are they your real names?"

"Yes, well we're actually Henry and Laurence but as you no doubt know Harry and Larry are the common names of the aforesaid." Larry took a sip of his beer.

"Of course, so do you live locally?"

"Not here in the village," said Harry, "We live in Penzance with our respective partners. Got a yard there where we keep all our stuff."

"Shall we sit down?" Sid nodded towards a vacant table, "My back's aching a bit tonight."

"Must be all the bending," Larry acknowledged, "Plumbing's renowned for it."

"Much like stonework," groaned Harry.

"You can say that again." Sid picked up his glass and crossed the bar with the brothers to a table by the door.

"So what do you want to know?" Sid asked as he pulled out a chair.

"Not really sure," admitted Larry, "but I suppose we're wondering if there's been much interest in the will and stuff like that."

"We've had a fair few descend on us but most were just hedging their bets I reckon because they've been and gone. One or two are definitely Joe's offspring though and they're still around."

"We thought it might raise a bit of interest especially getting TV coverage." Larry glanced around the bar curious to know if any persons present were confirmed offspring of Joe. To get an answer, he asked Sid.

"Not as far as I can see but they might be in later." Sid returned his gaze to the brothers, "So what about you two? Do you think you might be sons of his as well then?"

"Yeah, we do but we've no evidence to back it up," admitted Harry, "You see back in the swinging sixties our mother worked in this pub for a while and so we assume she got to know the locals. We were born in 1967 and after our birth, Mum was keen to get back to work which she eventually did by leaving us with Grandma but it wasn't this pub, by then she'd moved on to one in Penzance. Anyway, as she was driving home one really wet and miserable night having had several drinks I might add; she took a corner too fast, crashed the car and was killed instantly. She was just twenty one years old."

"Oh dear, that's terrible," Sid sympathised, "So you don't even remember her."

"No, we've nothing but a few old photos." Larry added.

"So what happened to you both?"

Harry sighed. "We were brought up by our grandparents and they did a damn good job. In later years we asked them about our dad but neither could tell us anything simply because they didn't know."

"Apparently Mum would never tell them," Larry confessed, "Grandma said she was very strong willed and independent."

"Obstinate too," added Harry.

"Yeah, a bit like us, I suppose."

"So what makes you think you might be Joe's boys?" Sid studied their faces to see if he could see any likeness to Irene, Norman or Biddy.

"Because the one thing Grandma could tell us was she reckoned our father's name was Joe," said Harry, "At least we're pretty sure that was the name she said."

"And I suppose your grandparents have since died so you can't ask them again."

"Yep, they've both been gone twenty years or more."

"Anyway, if you want to know for sure I suggest you take a DNA test. That's the only way to find out."

"How do we go about that?" Harry asked.

"You see that young lad over there playing pool?" The brothers nodded. "Well he works at the solicitor's office that are handling the will so he'll be able to advise you."

On Sunday morning, Irene and Martha went to church for although neither was particularly religious Irene needed comfort to help her come to terms with the brutal murder of her mother.

For a DNA test taken as requested by the police, confirmed that she was the daughter of the lady found in the oven; a result which enabled them to name the deceased as Geraldine Glover.

As they left the church they shook hands with Vicar Sam who greeted them cheerily. "Nice to see some new faces. Are you here for a winter break?"

"Not really," said Irene, "I suppose you could say we're here looking into our family history and my mother in particular."

"Well, if you need to see the church records at all I have access to them and it can be arranged."

Irene smiled weakly. "That's very kind of you but sadly they will be of no help. I already have my mother's birth and marriage certificates and as regards her death it appears that she was deprived of a Christian burial."

Sam's cheeks burned as realisation struck. "Oh, I'm so sorry," he stammered, "You must be the two ladies of whom Kitty our organist told me yesterday. Descendants of the young woman who was found in…in…the um…"

"Yes, we are," Irene spoke quickly to save the vicar's embarrassment.

"Well…um…if I can be of any help please don't hesitate to ask."

"Thank you, Vicar," said Martha, mildly amused by his discomfort, "it's been a shock but at least now Mum knows what happened to her mother. Well, not exactly what happened but she knows where she…um…oh dear."

Irene took Martha's hand. "Best not to think about it, my love." She then turned to Sam and looked into his eyes, "Actually, Vicar, you can help because now that she's found, Mother must have a proper funeral and I should like her to be buried here in the village. For despite what happened to her she did grow up here, was married here and probably even loved the place. Can that be arranged?"

"Of course. Shall I call on you?" Sam's composure had returned.

Irene brightened. "Yes, please do. We're staying at Sea View Cottage. Do you know of it?"

"Oh yes, seeing as it's within a stone's throw of the church."

"So it is, I'd lost my bearings for a minute." Irene looked over towards the church gate where the cottage roof was just visible on the other side of the road.

"Well if I may, would it be alright to call on you both at say three o'clock this afternoon or is that too soon?"

Irene nodded. "No, that's perfect. We hadn't any plans for the rest of the day and so we look forward to seeing you."

As the church clock struck three, Vicar Sam knocked on the door of Sea View Cottage. "Come in, Vicar," said Irene. Sam was delighted to see that she was in a much happier frame of mind.

"Please sit down," Irene waved her hand towards one of the two fireside chairs.

"Thank you."

"Tea, Vicar?" she asked, "or would you prefer coffee?"

"Tea would be lovely, thank you, but please call me Sam, nearly everyone else does."

"I'll make the tea, Mum," Martha jumped to her feet.

"No, no you sit down and entertain our guest, I'll not be long."

As Irene bustled off into the kitchen, Martha nervously sat back down in the other fireside chair. "I'm not quite sure how one entertains a vicar."

To her relief Vicar Sam's face broke into a huge grin. "Entertain me as you would anyone else," he laughed, "I'm quite human."

"Only quite?"

Sam felt uncomfortable under her gaze and was unable to think of an intelligent response. For Martha was very attractive and her eyes teased him.

"If I'm to entertain you as I would anyone else with whom I'm not well acquainted then I suppose we must discuss the weather."

Sam groaned. "Must we? It's been pretty miserable of late. Rain, rain and more rain."

"I can't disagree with that. So tell me, Sam, how long have you been the vicar here?"

"Not long, a couple of years, I think. I was in Devon before I came to Pentrillick."

"And would it be a silly question to ask if you like being a vicar?"

"No, not at all and the answer is yes I do. In fact I love it and love the people in this village too."

"What all of them?"

"Well…umm…"

"You don't need to answer that."

"Thank you."

"So does being a man of the cloth run in your family? I mean, was your father also a clergyman?"

Sam laughed. "No, my dad was a car mechanic and very good he was too. Well, he still is for that matter even though he's retired. How about you? What's your occupation?"

Martha smiled. "I'm a nurse."

"Ah, an admirable profession but it must be very trying at times."

"It is especially when one is faced with death," she smiled, "a bit like being a vicar, I suppose."

"Here we are, tea's ready," said Irene, as she carried in a tray on which stood three mugs of steaming tea, a bowl of sugar and slices of fruit cake, "I forgot to ask if you take sugar, Sam, and so brought the bowl."

"Thank you but I don't."

"Sweet enough already, eh?" Martha giggled.

As they drank their tea, Sam asked Irene if the police had released her mother's remains.

"Yes. I mean there's no reason for them to detain them, is there? Not after all this time so we can have a funeral whenever it's convenient to you and the undertakers."

"Okay, I'll give them a ring in the morning and arrange that."

"Thank you. I'd like it over and done with as soon as possible because we're only renting this place although we've been told we can extend our stay which we've already asked to do."

"I see," Sam put down his mug of tea and picked up a slice of cake, "Please don't think me indelicate but is it assumed by the police that your mother's life was taken by the baker, Joseph Williams or do they suspect someone else?"

"They suspect Joe," Irene whispered, "but he wasn't just the baker, Sam, he was my father."

Sam was taken back. "He was! Are you sure? I mean, how do you know?"

"Mother's DNA was a match with a man called Norman Williams who we are told is the son of Joseph the baker and it'll no doubt be a match with the DNA the solicitors have been authorised to verify the baker's offspring from."

"So, your mother was k…" Sam was unable to finish the sentence.

"Yes," sighed Irene, "my mother was killed by my biological father."

"But…but why?"

"That my dear, Sam, I doubt we shall ever know."

On Sunday evening, Bill, Sandra and the children were finally able to sleep in the Old Bakehouse for the first time. The upstairs rooms were all done, the wood burning stove was installed and the removal of the beds from the sitting room meant there was enough space to decorate the downstairs walls. Meanwhile, the baking room still had much work to be done to convert it fully into a kitchen and the dining room was habitable and just needed a lick of paint. The washing machine had been plumbed into the back porch but a partition wall still needed to be constructed in order to house the downstairs toilet and wash basin which Sid had already fitted in a corner.

"It feels like home now." Vicki stood at the foot of the stairs and took in a deep breath, "and I love the smell of the paint and the new carpets."

"I couldn't agree more and it's going to be fun putting up Christmas decorations this year," said Sandra, "we'll hang cards from the beams and have the tree standing in between the two windows."

"And lights around our front door," added Vicki.

Shortly after, Zac and Vicki went to their rooms but Kate seemed reluctant to follow.

"Anything wrong?" Sandra asked, "You don't look very happy. I thought you'd be keen to get upstairs and sleep for the first time in your very own room."

"Oh, I am. I love the house and my room, it's just…"

"It's just what?"

Kate's shoulders slumped. "It's just that I've never had a room all to myself before. It'll be weird not having Vicki to talk to."

"But I thought you wanted your own room," laughed Bill, "You were raving about it earlier."

"Yes, but that was before it got dark."

Sandra frowned. "But you're not afraid of the dark, surely, Kate."

"No, no, it's just that," she hesitated, "Do you believe in ghosts?"

"Ah, that's it, is it?" Bill chortled, "You think Geraldine Glover might come and back and haunt you."

Kate blushed. "It had crossed my mind, after all she did die here and so did Joe."

Sandra was more sympathetic than her husband. "Lots of houses have had people die in them, sweetheart including Primrose Cottage and you didn't feel uncomfortable there, did you? Anyway, if all houses in which people had died were haunted no-one would ever get any sleep."

"No, I suppose not."

Sandra stroked Kate's flushed cheek. "But if it'll make you feel better, leave your bedroom door open and we'll leave the landing light on all night and see how you get on but I promise you there's nothing to worry about."

Kate stood up. "Okay, thanks, Mum, I will. Goodnight."

As they heard Kate run up the stairs, Bill glanced at his wife who looked a little pale. "She hasn't got you worried too, has she?"

"No…but…well, there might be something in what she says, don't you think?"

Bill laughed. "If Geraldine Glover didn't haunt the place when she was cooped up in the oven I don't think she'll bother now that she's free and everyone knows her plight."

"Yes, I suppose you're right and if she was going to haunt anyone it'd have been old Joe seeing as how he murdered her."

"If he murdered her."

"Oh, don't let's go down that road again."

"I agree." Bill reached out and squeezed Sandra's hand. "Really, love, we've nothing to worry about here. Besides, this is a happy house now, especially since Auntie Het painted the front door bright yellow. Several people have told me they like it because it makes them smile."

"You're always so down to earth," laughed Sandra.

"I guess that's why you married me."

Sandra snuggled up beside him on the sofa. "I just wish I'd never seen that damn raven."

Bill laughed. "Or listened to your grandmother's silly tales."

"Hmm, perhaps you're right. Anyway, I've no need to worry because I know you'll protect us all against scary things."

"Scary things?"

"Yes, you know, ghosts, baddies or any murderers who might be lurking in the shadows."

"You read too many silly novels, Mrs Burton. Murderers indeed. There will be no more murders in this village. Mark my words."

Chapter Thirteen

It was cold, damp and very windy on Monday evening as Hetty walked down to the village after dark in torchlight with Albert, her Yorkshire terrier, on his lead. As she passed the Crown and Anchor she peeped in through the window to see if Zac was working behind the bar; when she saw that he wasn't she remembered that it was pool night and the team were away in one of the Helston pubs.

Because the evening was miserable and there were very few people outdoors, Hetty decided rather than to walk any further than the village, to let the dog have a good run around on the beach where she knew it would be possible for them to see in the glow of lights shining from buildings that overlooked the sand and shingle.

As she neared the alleyway which led down to the beach, she passed a lone figure. Unable to see the individual's face for her head was bowed low against the strong north-easterly wind, she nevertheless greeted the person in a friendly manner but received no more than a grunt in response. Assuming the person was unknown to her she turned into the alleyway which was a little more sheltered than the street.

As expected the beach was deserted except for a cat perched on a wall which seemed to be luring Albert to give chase. Hetty laughed as the small dog trotted across the sand and shingle, one eye on the cat, the other on the huge waves which he knew were in the habit of suddenly wetting his paws if he were not vigilant.

Hetty sat down on a bench. It was moist and she knew it would make her coat damp but it was only an old one and she considered it needed a wash anyway. To help keep warm she tucked her chin inside her scarf and folded her arms tightly; she then thought about Christmas and wondered if Bill and Sandra would have their new kitchen finished by then because due to the discovery of Geraldine Glover, work was well behind schedule.

Hetty pulled her woollen hat down over her ears to muffle the sound of the howling wind and the waves crashing onto the shore. The metal sign outside the beach shop, closed for the winter, added to the noise as it rattled and clattered in its frame accompanied by a tarpaulin flapping and snapping against the small boat it covered; a complete contrast, thought Hetty, to the stillness of a calm summer evening.

With the surrounding sounds slightly muffled, Hetty watched the lights of a distant ship on the horizon and while shuddering at the idea of being out at sea on such a cheerless night, she heard Albert barking. Concerned, she sat up straight. Was he chasing the cat or had another dog come onto the beach? She stood and cast her eyes in the direction of the little dog's barks. He was leaping on the spot and barking at something near the rocks at the end of the beach. Keen to put his mind at rest, Hetty hurried across the wet sand to where the little dog stood. When she saw the reason for his concern, her jaw dropped. Lying against the rocks, her legs soaked by the tumbling waves, was the body of a small woman. She wore a grey coat and was face down, one of her boots was missing and her exposed sock was entwined with a strand of seaweed. Hetty switched on her torch. Something appeared to be clasped in the woman's hand but it was not possible to see what. Hetty wanted to turn the body over to see if it was anyone she recognised but knew that she should not touch. However, knowing that it was important to establish whether or not the lady was alive, she searched for a pulse. To her amazement she felt a gentle throb. Realising time was of the essence she took her mobile phone from the pocket of her coat.

With trembling fingers she punched in 999 and asked for an ambulance and the police. Hetty then removed her coat and cardigan and covered the woman with both hoping that by doing so it might help prevent hypothermia setting in. She then sat down on the sand with Albert by her side and waited. As she shivered and her teeth chattered she prayed that the tide would slow down so that no more than the woman's legs would be submerged in sea water.

It seemed an eternity as she waited for help to arrive but in reality little more than ten minutes passed before she heard the welcome sound of sirens and saw the flashing blue lights. And as the team of men and women emerged from the vehicles being parked on the beach, she waved and called to them. With a police officer by her side, Hetty, now wrapped in a blanket, stood back and watched as the paramedics gently turned the body over. When she realised it was someone she knew, she gasped. The casualty was Bridget Barnes, the daughter of Joe and his first wife Cicely who had been adopted shortly after her birth.

Considering it was a Monday, that the pool team were away and that many people had been to work and had work the next day, the Crown and Anchor became very busy later that evening. Having heard the emergency vehicles' sirens the locals were keen to learn and spread the latest news. The most imaginative villagers on hearing of Bridget Barnes' plight insisted that she had been attacked and left for dead while those of a more down to earth disposition believed that she had been taken ill. The latter of the theories was eventually ratified by Bridget's husband, Geoff, who sent word from the hospital to Irene Hewitt with whom he and his wife had formed a friendship. Irene, who was in the pub with her daughter Martha informed the locals that Biddy had gone for a walk hoping to settle a bout of suspected indigestion which she had put down to having eaten a heavy lunch several hours earlier.

It was after nine when Hetty and Lottie put in an appearance. Hetty had been late getting home due to being questioned by the police and checked over by the paramedics who thought she might have suffered from the cold. Feeling better she was hopeful the pub would not be busy because she really just wanted to sit quietly and enjoy a large glass of wine which she hoped would steady her nerves and help her to sleep so that she might get the image of Biddy's bedraggled body from her mind. After the sisters had bought their drinks, Irene and Martha crossed the bar to commiserate with Hetty over her find.

Irene clutched Hetty's free hand. "It must have been a nasty shock for you."

"Yes, it was but she's in the best place now and I just hope she's going to be alright."

"I assume her husband is with her," said Lottie.

"Yes, he followed the ambulance to Truro and rang me from the hospital to tell us how she is. He seemed very calm, bless him, but then when I first met them I got the impression he was a level-headed individual."

"And how is she?" Hetty was almost afraid to ask.

"In a stable but serious condition and so hopefully she'll pull through."

"Any idea what they think happened?" Lottie asked.

Irene sat down. "As I've just been telling some of the locals it's thought she might have suffered a heart attack because Geoff said she was feeling unwell before she went out. Biddy assumed it was indigestion and thought a bit of fresh air and a walk might do her some good in spite of the miserable weather."

"So do they think it was an accident?" Hetty asked.

"Yes, without doubt. A heart attack, stroke or something along those lines."

Lottie sighed. "Thank goodness for that."

Hetty decided to say nothing at all because her instincts told her that Biddy had not been taken ill.

"While I'm here," said Irene, "would it be alright if I asked you a bit about umm, when you, well you know, found Mum? I mean, you were there at the time, weren't you?"

"Yes, both of us were and it was a great shock. I thought Lottie was going to faint when your moth…oh never mind." Hetty clammed up realising it would be indelicate to mention Geraldine's head rolling across the floor.

"I assume Sandra is your daughter-in-law, Lottie, who now lives in the Old Bakehouse?"

"Yes, that's right."

"So what would you like to know?" Hetty was curious.

"I just wondered if her handbag was with her. You see, when she left the house for the last time she took nothing with her which seemed odd back then. Now of course we know why. I mean, she wasn't intending to go anywhere, was she? But she still must have had her handbag with her because she never went anywhere without it. It just occurred to me that it might have been, well, you know with her when she was found."

The sisters both slowly shook their heads.

"There was nothing actually wrapped up with your mother in the eiderdown but there were two rings on one of her fingers and a pair of clip-on earrings and the remains of her outfit," said Lottie, "which the police still have."

"And a watch," Hetty added, "which had stopped at one o'clock."

"That's right and then separately to her there were a couple of cardboard boxes but they contained just general things from around the house although there was a dress and a pair of white sandals in one but definitely no handbag." For some reason Lottie glanced at her own handbag as she spoke.

"What was it like?" Hetty asked, "Your mother's handbag, I mean?"

"It was dark brown patent leather, capacious, with a bow on the side and a large brass clasp to close it with. Mum adored it and so did I. I'd love to see it again."

"Of course," said Lottie, "I'll get Sandra to look out for it because it might be somewhere else in the house although I think they've been through most of the stuff that was left behind now."

"And how about shoes?" Irene asked.

"Shoes! There weren't any shoes, were there, Het? Which I must admit does seem a little odd now I come to think of it."

"Mum loved her shoes, she must have had dozens of pairs. I used to clomp around the house in her older ones but was forbidden to put on any of the new ones." Irene smiled dreamily, "I'd wear some of Mum's old clothes too. When I was dressing up, I'd look in the mirror and see myself as a proper little lady instead of the gangly ten-year-old that I really was."

"So do you know what the missing shoes were like?" Hetty was curious.

"Brown patent leather to match her favourite handbag. I used to sit in the bottom of her wardrobe and smell her dresses after she had gone because they reminded me of her. They smelled so nice you see. Just as she used to. I played with her shoes too but I never dared try them on because it didn't seem right. I knew her shoes off by heart and the brown patent leather ones were the only pair that I could see were missing."

"So what did your father do with all your mother's things after she'd gone?" Lottie asked.

"He kept them until we moved to Portsmouth a couple of months later and then he chucked them out. If I remember correctly they all went to the village school for a jumble sale."

"That must have raised a few eyebrows," commented Hetty.

Irene shook her head. "It might have but everyone knew she'd gone and I suppose it was inevitable that she would have left some of her things behind."

"But no-one knew that she'd left everything," tutted Lottie.

"That's right and Dad said I must never tell anyone that that was the case. Looking back I think he was desperate not the lose face and liked to give the impression he'd sent her packing. He was a very proud man."

"So who looked after you when your mother left? While your father was working, I mean."

"He'd drop me off at school before he went to work and somehow managed to get away early so that he was home when I came out. It was only for a while anyway because shortly after we moved to Portsmouth where he met someone from his past and before long she'd moved in with us."

"And was she kind to you?" Lottie asked.

"Yes, she was and I really liked her. Her name was Madeleine and she had a great sense of humour which kept my spirits up. Sadly she died on my sixtieth birthday."

Chapter Fourteen

"So," said Debbie, when she arrived at Primrose Cottage on Tuesday morning to discuss the latest developments, "it looks very much to me as though someone is trying to bump off the competition as regards the money from the sale of the Old Bakehouse."

"My thoughts entirely," agreed Hetty, as she accompanied Debbie into the sitting room, "but everyone else seems to think that Biddy was taken ill, her husband included."

"That's what Gideon said but I disagree because I'm sure that if I suspected I was about to have a heart attack I would make sure I got well away from the water even if I had to stagger up the beach." Debbie sat down heavily as if to emphasise her point.

"Precisely."

"I'm glad you agree because as I said if she was attacked then the others with a claim on Joe's estate could be in danger too."

Hetty sat down at the table opposite Debbie. "It wouldn't surprise me if someone is planning to bump them off one by one."

"Poppycock," spluttered Lottie, "If anyone planned to do that, when he or she was the only one left he'd get nicked. Anyway, why are you so sure that it was attempted murder and not an accident? At present we don't know so you shouldn't jump to conclusions. Besides if it was attempted murder I'm sure we'd have heard by now and the place would be swarming with police doing house to house enquiries and stuff like that."

"But how do we know they haven't been doing house to house enquiries?" Hetty reasoned, "In fact they might be doing so right now but we wouldn't know because we're well away for the beach and the crime scene."

"Crime scene. Humph!" Lottie dusted the mantelpiece with unnecessary vigour in an attempt to hide her disdain.

"Well my money is on it being attempted murder." Hetty folded her arms to emphasise the point made, "What's more, I reckon there's a lot more to all this stuff to do with Joe and his will than meets the eye."

"And I still say you shouldn't jump to conclusions, either of you," hissed Lottie without turning her head.

"But you're jumping to conclusions by saying she was ill," snapped Hetty, "so I can't see the difference."

"Come on, come on, ladies, stop arguing," tutted Debbie, "it'll achieve nothing and we're all entitled to our own opinions."

"Alright," Hetty agreed, "so humour me, Lottie, and let's pretend for now that it was attempted murder and then if we hear anything to the contrary we'll review our ideas and I'll admit I was wrong."

Debbie nodded. "That's a reasonable compromise. So where shall we begin? I think we ought to make a list of all who might benefit from old Joe's will."

"I already have." Hetty produced a piece of paper from the pocket of her cardigan and handed it to Debbie. "Sadly it's very short but I don't think I've left anyone out."

Lottie tutted. "When did you write that?"

"This morning before you were up."

"Come and sit down with us, Lottie," begged Debbie, not wanting her friend to be left out, "there's no dust left on that mantelpiece now."

"Okay, but I'll go and get us all a coffee first. It should be ready by now." Lottie left the room.

Debbie looked at the sheet of paper. "Irene Hewitt, Norman Williams, Lucky Jim Bray and I see you have Biddy down too, poor soul. Not many to go on though, is it?"

"I think there are more," said Hetty, "but I don't know their names. Can you help?"

"Not really but I know that several have been and gone because their DNA tests were negative."

"I could hear what you were saying while I was in the kitchen and you've missed out the two chaps from Penzance," Lottie entered the room with a tray of coffee mugs.

"Two chaps from Penzance," repeated Debbie, "Who are they?"

"Ah, well remembered, Lottie," Hetty added the names to the list, "They're builders, Debbie, but not staying in the village. Sid was telling Bill and Sandra about them yesterday while he fitted an outside tap at the Old Bakehouse so that Sandra can water the garden when she's knocked it into shape. They're twins apparently and their names are Harry and Larry. Sid said they're really nice blokes."

As Lottie handed out the coffee mugs, there was a knock at the front door.

"I'll go since I'm on my feet."

On the doorstep stood their neighbour, Kitty.

"Hello, Kitty, come in, come in," Lottie stepped back to make room for Kitty to cross the threshold, "I've just made coffee. Would you like a mug?"

"Yes, please, it's quite chilly out."

"Okay, the others are in the sitting room. I'll be back in a jiffy."

"Hello, Kitty," Hetty stood up and pulled out a chair from beneath the table, "You're just in time. We're discussing likely suspects for Biddy's attempted murder."

"Assuming that is the case," added Debbie, knowing that Lottie was in earshot.

Kitty removed her coat and draped it on the back of the chair. "I didn't know anything about the Biddy incident until I was in the village just now where everyone's talking about it. How are you, Hetty? It must have been a bit traumatic for you."

"I'm fine, really I am. I got a bit cold waiting for the emergency services but I'm over the shock now."

As Kitty sat down she glanced at the names on the sheet of paper.

"That's a list of people who are in for a share of Joe's legacy," said Hetty, having followed Kitty's eyes, "We've made it because if Biddy's condition is the result of attempted murder then we think these people might be in danger too."

Kitty sighed. "I see your point and sadly it looks as though it was attempted murder and that's the reason for my visit. Well, that and to commiserate with you, Het."

"What!" Debbie shouted.

"I knew it," shrieked Hetty.

"That's terrible," said Lottie, as she returned to the room.

Debbie pushed the list to one side as Lottie put down Kitty's coffee along with a plate of biscuits.

"So what can you tell us?" Hetty asked, "How was she attacked?"

"It's reckoned the poor soul was suffocated and left for dead but I must admit that's pure speculation because no-one will know for sure 'til we've spoken to her husband. I know the police are definitely treating it as attempted murder though whatever the method of attack used."

"Are you sure it's definite?" Lottie sat down; her knees felt weak.

Kitty nodded. "Yes. As I walked along the main street this morning I met one of the chaps who puts together items in the *Pentrillick Gazette*. I asked him if there was any news and he told me what I've just told you. What's more there were several police cars parked along the street."

Lottie shook her head. "I concede defeat then but what a to-do."

"It certainly is. I met Pamela and Jim as I was walking up Long Lane and they asked if there had been anymore developments. When I told them what I've just told you Jim went as white as a sheet and said he thought it might be wise if they went home but Pamela wasn't bothered and said they must stay until after the deadline."

Hetty tutted. "That one's certainly determined to get her share."

"Do you know how Biddy is?" Debbie asked.

"She's still in a critical but stable condition and her husband is at her bedside. It's said the poor chap was devastated when he was told it was attempted murder."

"I'm not surprised," cried Lottie, "Poor Geoff."

"So, not only do we need to find out who murdered Geraldine Glover and put her in the oven we now need to find out who suffocated poor Biddy and left her for dead." Hetty picked up her mug of coffee.

"Well, one thing's for sure, with a sixty year time span it certainly won't be the same person," chuckled Lottie.

"No, it won't and I don't think many have any doubts as to who killed Geraldine," said Debbie, "Even the police think it was Joe. But Biddy, well, it could be anyone although my money is on it being one of her new found siblings."

"But they're all really nice," insisted Kitty.

"In which case perhaps there is one we've yet to hear about." As Hetty spoke a sudden image flashed across her mind. "Oh, my goodness, I've just remembered something. Last night before I found Biddy I met someone along the main street. I said hello but whoever the person was just grunted in response and carried on walking. To be honest I've no idea who it was but we were near to the alleyway so it could easily have been the attacker coming up from the beach."

Lottie was shocked. "For goodness sake, you must be able to remember something about the person, Het. I mean, what was he wearing? How tall was he?"

"I really don't know. My head was bowed because of the wind. I had no reason to take in any detail and I only saw his feet anyway."

"Okay, so what was on his feet?"

"A pair of flashy white trainers with blue squiggles on the sides."

"Well, that's something," conceded Kitty. "You must tell the police."

Chapter Fifteen

In the evening, Hetty and Lottie gave bingo a miss; Debbie was unable to go because it was her husband Gideon's birthday and she was taking him out for a meal. Instead the sisters walked down to the Crown and Anchor hoping to hear more news.

Earlier in the day, Hetty had told the police that she had seen someone in the vicinity of the beach on the night of Biddy's attack but because she was unable to give a description of any kind, other than that the person in question had worn flashy white trainers with blue squiggles down the sides, she conceded her input was next to useless.

As they entered the pub they saw that the bar was very busy. "Listen to the chatter." Hetty looked around as she unzipped her coat. "You grab that table, Lottie before someone else does and I'll get the drinks."

Behind the bar, Tess Dobson was working alongside licensees, Ashley and Alison Rowe.

"Judging by the loud chatter I'd make a wild guess and say most are trying to work out who tried to kill poor Biddy," said Hetty, after she had ordered two glasses of red wine.

Tess tutted. "Not like you to be behind with the news, Het."

"Behind. What do you mean?"

"There's been an arrest." Tess left Hetty wondering while she stepped away and poured the wine.

"Who?" Hetty looked Tess in the eye as she stood the two glasses on the bar.

"Irene Hewitt. You know, the daughter of the woman who was found in your nephew's oven. She was arrested earlier this evening." Tess kept her voice low because Ashley the landlord didn't like his staff to gossip while at work.

"But that's ridiculous," hissed Hetty. "There must be a mistake. Irene is lovely." She took money from her purse.

"That's as maybe but the police found a silver necklace in Biddy's hand which has been identified as Irene's. In fact Irene confirmed it herself. It's assumed Biddy pulled it from her neck during the attack."

Hetty's jaw dropped as she recalled seeing something clasped in Biddy's hand. After Tess gave her the change from a ten pound note, she returned to her sister in a daze.

The following morning dawned dull but dry with a strong autumnal wind blowing from the east. Looking out into the back garden of Primrose Cottage, Albert sat on the granite doorstep and watched the leaves as they fluttered over the boundary wall from Ginny and Alex's cherry tree and settled on the pond and surrounding lawns and flower beds.

Inside the cottage, the sisters sat at the table in their sitting room eating breakfast and discussing the goings-on in the village.

"Fancy a trip to the care home?" Hetty suddenly asked

"Who to visit? Charlie or Nellie?"

"Both if they're free."

"Yes, why not. We told Charlie we'd go back so we must keep our word. He might even have remembered something by now."

"That's what I'm thinking. I also want something to occupy my mind other than Irene's arrest. I'm struggling to come to terms with that because it makes no sense."

"I couldn't agree more."

At the care home they found Charlie sitting in the same chair as on the previous visit. His face lit up when he saw them and he eagerly shook their hands. As they pulled up chairs and sat down in front of him Charlie reached beneath his armchair and pulled out a photograph album.

"I've kept this in here to show you because I knew you'd be back." He opened it on the first page and passed it to Lottie who sat nearest to him; she placed it on her lap.

"Audrey made up the album," Charlie said with pride, "and as you can see she'd written underneath every picture the names of the people in it and the dates as well. Audrey was very meticulous."

"So I see," Hetty glanced at the album where a young Charlie smiled at the camera alongside his wife, "and I have to say you were a very handsome man when you were young."

"Oh, don't you think I'm handsome now then?"

"Yes, yes, of course you are, it's just…"

"Only kidding," he chuckled, "you must forgive me but I've spent my life pulling the legs of folks and not everyone sees the funny side."

When Lottie turned the page they saw a black and white picture of a group of school children posing in the playground and dated 1945. "Was that taken before or after the war ended?"

"Just after. I remember it well because I was twelve by then that's why I'm on the back row with the big children."

Hetty pointed to a young girl with dark hair. "And next to you it says Nellie who I assume is the midwife. She said she was at school with you."

"That's right and the lad on the other side of me is my best mate Frank. Well I should say was because he's dead now more's the shame."

"Frank Bell," said Lottie looking at the bright eyed boy next to Charlie, "Would he by any chance be related to Ding…I mean Douglas Bell who rings the church bells?"

"Yep, Douglas is Frank's grandson. He's not here now though. Someone told me he's gone gallivanting off somewhere or other teaching kids. Been gone a while I think."

"He's back now," said Hetty, "we saw him in the pub the other evening."

"He is? Good, hopefully he'll come and see me then," Charlie looked back at the album, "Can you spot my Audrey?"

"Yes, but I probably wouldn't be able to do so were the children not named," admitted Lottie.

"Eve," Hetty pointed to the girl next to Audrey, "Would that be the same Eve who married Joe the baker?"

"Yep, the very one and if you look on the front row at the little ones you'll see her sister, Alice."

"Well I never," sighed Lottie, "what a pretty little girl she was."

"And she still was when she grew up," chuckled Charlie, "she were a cracker in her day and had us blokes fighting over her. In the end she married a chap from Porthleven though and so moved away. I don't think I've seen her since. In fact I don't even know if she's still alive."

"Oh, she's alive and well, we saw her not long ago and she's still living in Porthleven although she's a widow now." Lottie turned to the next page of the album.

"She is? Fancy that. I knew Eve had gone, God rest her soul because Nellie told me. She also said Eve's little boy's been back to the village. I bet he don't recognise the place."

Hetty smiled. "Not so little now though that he's sixty two."

"Is he really? Well, yes, I suppose he'd have to be. How time flies."

That same morning, Vicar Sam having heard of Irene's arrest walked down to Sea View Cottage hoping he might be able to offer a few words of comfort to her daughter Martha who he realised would now be all alone in the village. To his dismay there was no-one home and so he walked down to the beach for a stroll along the shore before he returned home to the Vicarage. As he neared the sea he saw a lone figure sitting on one of the benches; she wore no coat and her dark hair was tousled by the sea breeze; when she heard his feet crunching across the shingle she turned around.

"Martha. I've just been to call on you but you weren't in." He pointed to the back of Sea View Cottage.

She half smiled. "No, and that's because I'm here."

"Yes, how silly of me." He walked closer. "May I?" He pointed to the empty space on the bench.

"Of course." Martha shuffled along to give him more room.

"I'm very sorry to hear of your mother's arrest. I'm sure it's all a big mistake but if there's anything I can do, anything at all, please don't hesitate to ask."

Martha looked out to sea. "At this stage I don't think there's much anyone can do. Not even your God. The police are convinced Mother did it and they have evidence to back up their conviction." She turned her head and looked Sam in the eye, "As for me, I'm confused, angry and bitter even. But I can control my emotions and I'll not let the situation wear me down. I just wish Mum was stronger."

"Is there anyone you can get to come and stay with you? Brothers, sisters, friends? I can't bear to think of you having to go through this on your own."

"That's very sweet but please don't worry and yes, I do have someone. My father is on his way down here as we speak. He should be here in an hour or two."

"Thank goodness."

"He's very level headed, you know, and I have faith he'll be able to sort it all out. He should, he's a lawyer."

Sam sighed. "That's a relief."

"Yes, yes, it is."

"Do you want to talk about it? I mean, would it help at all?" Sam found it difficult not to fidget.

Martha shook her head. "If you don't mind I'd rather not. I'm trying to work it out, you see, and daft as it might sound, watching the waves as they tumble on the shore and hearing the shingle shift beneath the waves is very therapeutic and actually all the help I need."

"So would you rather I left you in peace?"

"Would you think me ungracious if I said yes?"

"No, of course not." Sam stood. "I understand. I'll go then but please remember if you need a shoulder to cry on or someone to talk to, I'm not far away."

"I'll remember that. Thank you, Sam. You're very sweet."

After gently squeezing her hand, he left. And as Martha heard the fading sound of his feet crunching across the shingle until it was no longer audible, tears began to trickle down her pale cheeks.

Chapter Sixteen

On Wednesday afternoon, Hetty and Lottie learned that Irene's husband had arrived in the village.

"His name is Jack," declared Kitty, the informant, who had called round to see them, "I'm so glad Martha is no longer alone. I saw Sam just now and he said he went to see her this morning after he'd heard they had taken her mother away and needless to say the poor girl was and is extremely upset."

"Hardly surprising." Hetty found it hard to keep the anger she felt from her voice.

"We think Irene is innocent," said Lottie, "and that she has been framed."

"There's no question about it," spluttered Hetty, "The two women got on really well and it's bonkers to even think that Irene would hurt Biddy."

Kitty sat down. "Framed, but how and by who? I mean, there's no doubt in anyone's mind as to whether or not the necklace in Biddy's hand belonged to Irene. Both she and Martha have identified it."

"Someone might have one the same," reasoned Lottie, "I daresay it'll be mass produced."

"No doubt the locket is, yes, but not the picture inside it. It's a picture of Geraldine, you see. Irene cut it from an old photograph after her mother left. The locket had been a present from her parents on her tenth birthday."

Hetty felt her heart rate increase. "But that's ridiculous. There has to be a simple explanation and by hook or by crook we'll endeavour to find out what it is. I just wish I knew where to start looking."

"Well, I hope you're right," said Kitty, "I really, really do."

After Kitty left, the sisters walked down to the Old Bakehouse in order to see the sitting room which Sandra had messaged the day before to say she had finished decorating. The room was cosy and warm despite its size.

"It's beautiful," Lottie ran her hand over the wall, "and I love the embossed wallpaper. You have done well."

"Thank you, I've enjoyed doing it. Next job will be the dining room, but I won't start that until Basil and Mark have finished the kitchen, and it only wants a lick of paint anyway."

Hetty looked at the bare solid floor. "You just need the carpet in here now to finish it off."

"That's right and we've ordered one but before we can get it laid we need to sort out these pianos. Which one would you like, Het? They both need tuning because your old one took a knock or two during the move."

"I really don't mind, so you choose."

"Well I think the one that was already here goes with the décor better than yours simply because it's lighter in colour."

"That's fine with me. In fact it'll be nice to have my old one back. I was only twenty-nine when I bought it so I've known it for quite a while."

"Do you know anyone with a vehicle suitable to move it?" Sandra wondered.

Hetty shook her head. "No but I'll ask around and try and find the name of a piano tuner at the same time."

Basil who had just come in after a trip to the builders' merchants heard what was said through the open door. "I'll shift the piano for you if you like."

Sandra's face lit up. "Would you? I'd really appreciate it if you could."

"No problem. Just let me know when you're ready."

"Bless you. We will, thank you."

As Basil returned to his work Hetty noticed a gardening book on the coffee table. "Have you started on the jungle out the back yet, Sandra?"

"Actually I have but nothing drastic. I cleared part of the area outside the French doors and was delighted to find paving slabs underneath the weeds. They might need a bit of pointing but I reckon they'll clean up well and make a nice little patio area."

"Lovely, and the ideal spot for sitting out at the end of a summer's day," said Hetty, "because it'll get the evening sun."

"That's what Bill said. I also did a bit of weeding around a choked fuchsia and made a friend at the same time: a little robin which clearly approved of my efforts. Bill's going to repair the old bird table when he has a day off, then we'll be able to feed him and his friends."

"You'll get hours of entertainment from it when you do. We love watching the birds on the one we have out the front, don't we, Het?"

"Yes, better than the television most days."

"Talking of birds, how is Biddy doing?"

Hetty frowned. "She's coming along fine but what does that have to do with birds?"

Sandra looked sheepish. "Nothing I suppose. It's just that on the night she was attacked I had to go outside to get my phone from the car and that wretched raven was on our roof again."

The sisters stayed at the Old Bakehouse for a cup of tea and then made their way home. As they passed Sea View Cottage on the other side of the road they saw an unfamiliar car parked alongside the one they knew belonged to Martha.

"That must be Irene's husband, Jack's car," Hetty pointed to the black BMW, "Shall we pop over and introduce ourselves?"

Lottie was hesitant. "Do you think we ought? I mean, they might not want to see anyone. I'm sure that if I was in their shoes I'd want to be left alone."

"If they think Irene's guilty then yes that might be the case but I bet you, like us, they know she's innocent."

Lottie stopped walking. "I agree but as Kitty said the evidence against her is pretty solid which makes it all very awkward."

"Maybe but I'd like to hear what they have to say."

"Okay, we'll knock but if we feel we're unwelcome I suggest we leave at the first possible opportunity."

"Yes, I'll go along with that." Hetty looked both ways along the street to ensure that it was safe to cross.

Martha answered the door and to Lottie's relief she seemed genuinely pleased to see them. "Please come in. It's good to see friendly faces."

An elderly man stood as Martha led them into the sitting room.

"Dad, these two ladies are Hetty and Lottie. Remember I was just telling you about them. It's Lottie's son and his family who are now living in the Old Bakehouse."

He stepped forward and shook hands with the sisters in turn. "Delighted to meet you both. I'm Jack Hewitt." He waved his hand towards the sofa, "Please sit down."

"Thank you," said Hetty, "I hope you don't think it rude of us to call at what must be a very difficult time for you both."

Jack shook his head. "No, not at all. Talking helps us try and make sense of all this and as you can imagine we're one hundred percent sure that Irene is innocent."

"Would you like a cup of tea?" Martha asked.

Lottie shook her head. "No thank you, we've just come from Bill and Sandra's and had one less than an hour ago."

Martha sat down in the fireside chair opposite her father.

"How is Irene faring?" Lottie felt her voice tremble.

Jack plumped up the cushion behind his back. "She seems reasonably okay. Like us she knows she's innocent and has faith that the truth will come out eventually. Although God only knows how we'll be able to prove it."

"Oh, that's good to hear," Lottie felt there might be a glimmer of hope, "that she has faith the truth will come out, I mean."

"Has she been charged yet?" Hetty asked.

Jack shook his head. "No, but we're expecting she will be any time now. They can only hold her for so long."

"But surely she must have an alibi," reasoned Lottie.

Martha sighed deeply. "Sadly she doesn't. It was my turn to cook the dinner on Monday evening and so Mum decided to go for a walk to get some fresh air and work up an appetite while I was busy in the kitchen. She told the police and me that she just walked through the village and then on the way back she sat down on a bench in the churchyard for a while which was sheltered from the wind. She found the graves of her maternal grandparents over there the other day, you see, and said it made her feel in touch with her roots. She was back within the hour of leaving, I can vouch for that and she vows that she didn't go anywhere near the beach."

"And did she seem normal when she got back?" Hetty asked.

Martha was hesitant. "Not normal as in how she was before we came to Pentrillick but I suppose she was much the same as she's been since we learned of her mother's fate."

"And she doesn't have any reason to want Biddy dead anyway," scoffed Jack, "I mean, no way was Biddy involved in the death of Irene's mother so there's no motive there at all. And as for suggesting she wanted a bigger share of the inheritance, well, that's absurd. We're not short of a bob or two and the dear soul isn't motivated by money anyway."

"We believe she was framed," blurted Martha, "as Dad said there's no way Mum would have tried to kill Biddy or anyone else for that matter and it's daft to say she would. What's more, she liked Biddy, after all they are half-sisters."

"Yes, I suppose they are," conceded Hetty, "I hadn't thought of that and for what it's worth we think Irene was framed too."

"So, what do you think happened?" Lottie asked.

"We think the person who attacked Biddy broke in here, stole Mum's necklace and then placed it in Biddy's hand after he or she thought they had killed her."

Lottie gasped. "That would mean it was premeditated."

Jack nodded. "Exactly."

"But surely you'd know if someone had broken in," reasoned Hetty.

"Not if they used a key," said Martha, "You see, the key to the house was left under a flower pot by the conservatory door at the back of the house when we arrived and so whenever we went out we left it there so we wouldn't lose it and the chances are that someone knew that."

Hetty's jaw dropped. "We stayed here for a holiday a few years ago before we moved to the village and the key used to be left under a plant pot out the back then too. Of course the cottage belonged to someone else then, I can't remember his name but Brett Baker, the current owner, didn't buy it 'til earlier this year."

"Do you know Brett?" Lottie asked, "It's just that the cottage is usually empty when he's not here."

Martha shook her head. "No, we saw an advert on-line and booked our stay here through that. The advert said the cottage was available for a few weeks in the winter which was ideal. In fact we rang the agents this morning and asked them if we could extend our stay yet again. We'd already done it once, you see. They said yes because no-one will be here 'til the owner comes down at Christmas."

"I see. So going back to the necklace. You reckon someone got in using the key you'd left beneath the plant pot and then stole it?" Hetty reiterated, "Necklace that is, not the plant pot."

Martha nodded. "Yes."

"That's unnerving," admitted Lottie, "because it suggests the thief might be a local person."

"When did your mother last wear the necklace?" Hetty asked.

Martha shrugged her shoulders. "I've no idea."

"The reason I ask is because I'm wondering if someone saw her wearing it and thought it would be the ideal thing to plant in Biddy's hand."

"Could be but I think it's more likely he or she just looked for anything that might incriminate Mum."

"What a ghastly mess," tutted Lottie, "There are some horrible people in the world."

"There are," Hetty agreed, "and I can't help but wonder now if the person I saw before I found Biddy was in fact the person responsible for Biddy's attack."

"You saw someone. What did he look like?" Jack was on the edge of his seat.

"Sadly I can't say. It was a very windy night and I had my head bowed. I spoke to the person but he just grunted in response and the only thing I noticed were his feet and the flashy white trainers he wore."

"With blue squiggles down the sides," Lottie added.

"That's interesting," mused Jack, "because even though you've no idea who it was it does prove that there was someone else about that evening."

"You've obviously told the police," quizzed Martha.

"Yes I have."

"And as far as you know he or she wasn't someone you knew?"

"Correct and it certainly wasn't your mother."

Martha smiled. "Yes, there's no question about that because Mother doesn't even own a pair of trainers."

Jack leaned back in his chair. "Oh well, our only hope now then is that Biddy will soon be able to talk to the police and tell them what really happened."

"In which case," said Martha, "I pray that Biddy's memory was not harmed by the trauma."

Chapter Seventeen

On Thursday evening, Hetty and Lottie walked down to the Crown and Anchor to meet up with their friend, Debbie, where they planned to tell her of their meeting with Jack and Martha. However, before the subject was even broached, Lottie spotted someone they knew chatting at the bar to her son, Bill.

"Norman's back." She beckoned the two men to join them.

"You didn't tell me Norman was back in Pentrillick, Bill," admonished Lottie.

"That's because I didn't know myself until I walked in here twenty minutes ago."

"I only arrived this afternoon," Norman acknowledged, "I thought I better come down to see what's going on. Aunt Alice rang me yesterday, you see, to say she's heard on the local news that there had been an attempted murder in Pentrillick and it seemed to be connected with Joe, or should I say my late father."

"Yes, a rum do that," tut-tutted Lottie, "We're trying to make sense of it because we're convinced the person they've arrested for the attack is completely innocent."

"So Bill's been telling me."

Hetty looked around. "No Jackie?"

"No, she couldn't get the time off work at such short notice because they've got a big party on where she works this weekend but she hopes to get down for a few days next week. Thankfully I've a very understanding boss and he said to take as long off as I want."

"I'm pleased to hear it." Hetty patted his hand affectionately, "and it's good to see you back."

"Yes, I wish Jackie was here though because she makes me laugh and she's longing to fathom out what's going on here."

"Aren't we all?" Bill sighed.

"Sit down," commanded Lottie, "you both look awkward standing there."

The two men did as they were told.

"Are you staying at the hotel again?" Hetty asked.

"Yes, I'm here for a whole fortnight this time and hopefully while I'm here we'll be able to get to the bottom of all this. I'm not alone by the way. I've brought Mum with me."

Hetty and Lottie's jaws dropped simultaneously.

"But Eve…your mum…" muttered Lottie.

"Oh yes, you are right she *is* dead. It's her ashes I have with me. I had a word with your vicar when I was last here, you see, and I'm going to have them buried in your churchyard. Jackie and I decided it'd be a nice thing to do when we were down before."

"Quite right too," Hetty concurred, "after all Eve's family are all resting there now."

"All except for me," chuckled Norman, "but I see no reason why I shouldn't end up over there as well and back in the bosom of my family but I hope it won't be for a good few years yet."

"Talking of family, I was just telling Norman about the boxes of Joe's memorabilia that we've put aside for him," said Bill, "and of course Joe's paintings."

"I'm really looking forward to going through them. I've nothing from my past at the moment other than a few certificates and a handful of black and white photos taken of me as I was growing up."

"Well, there are several pictures amongst Joe's stuff," said Lottie, "and it'd be nice if you could put names to some of the faces."

Norman shook his head. "But I didn't know any of them so I'll only be able to recognise Mum. That's not a problem though. I'll take them down to Aunt Alice and see if she can help."

"Good idea," Hetty agreed.

"And if she can't remember who's who you must go along to the care home to see Charlie Pascoe and Nellie Gibson," insisted Lottie, "Charlie's the builder who bricked up the oven and Nellie has lived in the village all her life and used to be a midwife so both should be able to identify some of the faces. In fact Charlie was showing us his photograph album only the other day and some of them were of your mum and Aunt Alice."

"Really! I'll try and get round to doing that then."

Hetty suddenly remembered the piano. "I'm glad you're here, Norman because there's a piano in the Old Bakehouse and we wondered who played, whether it was your mother or Joe."

"There are two now," chuckled Bill.

"Two?" repeated Norman.

"We brought one with us. It used to belong to Auntie Het but she gave it to Kate when she and Mum moved down here."

"And I'm going to have it back," Hetty added.

"I see and it's funny you should mention a piano because when I went to see Aunt Alice she asked me if I played. I don't I might add but Mum did although not very well. Alice said it was quite handy for Mum because next door to the Old Bakehouse lived a piano tuner who also gave her lessons."

"Really! Perhaps he's still there." Hetty was very optimistic.

"I doubt it," laughed Lottie, "not after all these years."

"I wonder where that was then," pondered Bill, "because on one side of us is the hairdressers and the other the road. Although I suppose she might have meant the house next to us in Goose Lane. It makes it a bit complicated living on a corner."

"Anyway, if he's not there I must remember to ask Kitty if she knows of a good piano tuner which I suppose she must since she plays."

"Failing that you can ask Ashley or Alison because there's a piano in here as well." Lottie nodded towards the piano in the corner of the bar.

The following morning, Kitty called round to Primrose Cottage with the news that Biddy had regained consciousness the previous evening and had been able to talk to the police.

"Hurrah," sang Lottie, as she showed Kitty into the sitting room, "now we'll get to the truth and Irene should be released."

As she sat in a fireside chair, Kitty shook her head. "Sadly that's not to be though because believe it or not, Biddy says the person who attacked her was wearing dark trousers and a light coloured jacket; had dark, shoulder length, curly hair and wore glasses with dark rims."

Hetty slumped down on the sofa. "What! Surely not."

Kitty looked downcast. "That's what I said when I heard. I mean, we all know that Irene often wears dark trousers and a light coloured jacket, has dark, shoulder length, curly hair and wears dark rimmed glasses."

"I don't believe it," Lottie sat down heavily on the sofa beside her sister, "Something's wrong somewhere."

"Did she say what shoes she was wearing?" Hetty asked.

"It wasn't mentioned."

Lottie looked at Hetty. "You're thinking of the person you saw that night near the alleyway."

"Yes, I am. No way was that person Irene because she would have spoken if it was."

"Did Biddy get a look at her attacker's face?" Lottie asked.

Kitty shook her head. "No, because it was dusk and it all happened so quickly. She just remembers sensing that someone was behind her, she turned around and then within seconds everything had gone black and she couldn't breathe."

"And so it might not have been a woman and could just as easily have been a man." Hetty was grasping at straws.

"I suppose even that's possible," Lottie agreed, "but surely this description on top of the necklace being in Biddy's hand and the fact that she's entitled to a share of Joe's legacy and might want a bigger share for herself will give the police reason enough to consider they have sufficient evidence to charge her now."

Kitty sighed deeply. "Yes, and that's the other thing I was going to tell you. Irene was formally charged last night and is due to appear in court on Monday afternoon."

Hetty was so shocked that all thoughts of asking about a piano tuner slipped her mind.

That same morning, Sandra walked a few yards down the street to the antiques shop where she hoped to make a few purchases of things to give the Old Bakehouse the final touch. Her main search was for a coal scuttle for although having a wood burner meant they would not be burning solid fuel, Sandra thought it would look nice and be somewhere to store brushes, matches, heat resistant gloves and other bits and bobs needed for a fire.

Ginny was in the shop when she arrived; Alex she was informed was out in his part-time capacity as a driving instructor.

"Ah, and that reminds me," said Sandra, "After Christmas would Alex be able to give Zac some driving lessons? He started to learn a year ago but gave up after a while. He wants to start again now though and it'd be nice if he could get his test over and done with before the holiday season next summer."

"No problem. Let Alex know when he's ready and we'll take it from there."

"We'll do that but what I actually came in for was a coal scuttle."

"A coal scuttle, now that we can do, in fact I'm pretty sure we have three."

Ginny led Sandra across the room to where several items relating to the hearth filled a corner.

Sandra picked up the larger of the three coal scuttles and looked at it from all angles. "Perfect, and you have some bellows as well. We shouldn't need them but I think they'd look nice on the opposite side to the coal scuttle to balance it out if you see what I mean."

"I do and I agree but then I suppose I would say that, wouldn't I?"

Sandra smiled. "Yes, anyway I'll take both."

Ginny leaned back on a chest of drawers. "How's the Old Bakehouse coming along?"

"Very well, especially now we're sleeping there. The downstairs rooms have yet to be finished but the upstairs is all done." As she spoke she caught sight of a matching Victorian wash bowl and jug. "Oh, they are beautiful and would look perfect in our bathroom. I could stand them on the small chest and fill the jug with flowers. We've painted it all white so a bit of colour will brighten it up."

"You must like jugs then because a little bird told me that you intend to hang jugs and teacups from the beams."

"Teacups alongside their saucers in the sitting room and jugs in the kitchen, although the kitchen won't be finished for a while yet."

"No, I suppose it was inevitable that the discovery of poor Geraldine Glover would hold things up."

Sandra smiled. "I bet you and Alex never imagined when you agreed to be the executors of Joe's will that it would open up such a can of worms."

"We most certainly didn't and now one of the beneficiaries has been assaulted as well. I have to confess I'll not be sorry when we get to midnight on November the thirtieth and can wind this all up."

As Sandra cast her eyes over other items on display she caught sight of a small dog curled up and asleep in a basket beneath a dining table. "Oh, bless him. Is that Joe's little dog?"

"Yes, that's him and his name is Crumpet."

On hearing his name, Crumpet pricked up his ears, stretched and stepped out onto the wooden floor.

"What a sweetheart," Sandra knelt down to stroke the little dog's head, "What will become of him?"

"I don't know as it's yet to be decided."

"Well, if there are no claims we'd be more than happy to give a home. The girls would love him. They said only the other day that they wanted a dog."

"That might be the best idea, after all he knows the Old Bakehouse having lived there since he was a puppy."

Sandra stood up and took her purse from her handbag. "Very true. Anyway, how much do I owe you?"

Ginny totted up the total.

Sandra paid with her debit card and gathered up her purchases. "Oh, and before I forget, do you know if anyone in the village tunes pianos? It's just that we have two. One we brought with us and the other which belonged to Joe although it seems it was his wife who played it. They both need tuning anyway and then one of them needs to be shifted up to Primrose Cottage. We need it done pretty soon so that we get the sitting room carpet fitted."

Ginny nodded. "Do you know the two ladies who work in the charity shop?"

"Yes, I've seen them a couple of times."

"Well one of them is called Daisy and her husband used to tune pianos and I think he still does. He's retired now of course but I'm sure he'll be able to help especially as you're in the village."

"Was that his occupation then before he retired?"

"No, no, he was an engineer but pianos are his passion and he did the tuning part time."

"Sounds ideal then, I'll get Bill's mum or his Aunt Het to have a word with Daisy as they like an excuse to go to the charity shop."

Chapter Eighteen

Inside the workshop at the back of the Old Bakehouse, Bill, happy to have a day off work, stood at an old work bench busily mending the broken bird table with pieces wood he'd found lying around. It didn't take long and by mid-afternoon it looked as good as new and was back in the garden where it could be seen from the French doors in the sitting room. Satisfied with his workmanship, Bill returned indoors to tell his wife it was ready for any bird goodies she might have. Sandra, keen to see her robin back, crushed some peanuts and then scattered them, along with assorted seeds over the table; she and Bill sat down on the couch, cups of tea in hand ready to observe any birds which chose to dine on Bill's handiwork. To their delight, the robin was the first to arrive.

"So," declared Hetty, as she sat at the table in Primrose Cottage with Debbie and Kitty the following morning, "we need to try and establish who might have a motive for killing Biddy so that we can get poor Irene released."
"Perhaps it was a case of mistaken identity," reasoned Kitty.
"You mean someone thought Biddy was someone else?"
"Yes."
"Hmm, it's possible I suppose but why go to the trouble of making it look like the attacker was Irene?"
"Perhaps they didn't and the fact the attacked wore similar clothes to Irene is pure coincidence." The thought had only just occurred to Lottie.

Kitty shook her head. "No, you've forgotten about the necklace."

Lottie sighed deeply. "Yes I had, so it really does look as though Irene was framed."

"Exactly," snapped Hetty, "So we need to urgently find someone with a strong motive who would want Biddy out the way and who was prepared to let Irene take the blame."

"Which takes us back to Joe's will and the share out of his legacy."

Kitty frowned. "It just occurred to me. Would the fact that Irene might end up a convicted criminal prevent her from receiving her share of the inheritance?"

"I don't see why it should," said Lottie.

Hetty nodded her head. "I agree, and so why bother to frame her?"

"Good point and so I think we ought to try and come up with a different motive because the Joe's will theory makes no sense at all," reasoned Debbie.

"But what could it be? No-one in the village knew Biddy until she turned up here the other day and the same goes for Irene so it has to be connected to the legacy." Kitty closed her eyes tightly as though expecting a vision.

"I agree, so how about Norman? Might he have wanted all the money for himself?" Hetty suggested.

"I hardly think so, Het," snapped her sister, "after all he didn't even know Joe was his real father until after his mother died. Besides he's a really nice bloke."

"And he wasn't here when Biddy was attacked anyway," Debbie reminded them.

"What's more, he's just inherited the house he lives in so is probably quite comfortably off anyway." Lottie was still clearly annoyed by Hetty's suggestion.

"Okay, how about Lucky Jim?" Hetty didn't like being called 'guy'.

Debbie frowned. "I don't think so because I get the impression from Jim that he couldn't care less about any inheritance and finds the whole thing rather sordid."

"I agree but what about his mother, Pamela?" said Lottie, "The woman's very pushy and seems determined to get her hands on any money that might come their way."

Kitty gasped. "What's more, she has dark curly hair."

"And she also has a light coloured jacket," squealed Hetty.

"She doesn't wear dark rimmed glasses though, does she?" stressed Debbie, "In fact I've never seen her wearing glasses at all."

"Ah, but they might have been magnifying reading glasses." Lottie reasoned they could be purchased anywhere in all styles, shapes and sizes.

Hetty's face lit up. "And the money *would* definitely be her motive so that sounds good to me."

"In which case she must have broken into Sea View Cottage and stolen Irene's necklace," shrieked Debbie, "and that's more than feasible since she's here in the village at the moment. I mean, she's no doubt sussed out where people are staying."

"Does she have an alibi for the night Biddy was attacked?" Kitty wondered.

"If she does it'll most likely be Jim, in which case we need to establish how sound it is. Meanwhile, Pamela goes to the top of the suspect list." Hetty took the crumpled piece of paper from her cardigan pocket and rearranged the suspect's names.

Lottie looked at the clock on the mantelpiece. "Does the charity shop close for lunch?"

"Yes," said Kitty, "between one and two."

"I thought so. It's just we need to go and see Daisy about her husband tuning the two pianos at the Old Bakehouse. Sandra rang last night to say Ginny had recommended him so we need to book him as soon as possible. That's assuming he still tunes pianos. Do you know if he does, Kitty?"

"Yes, and very good he is too. He's been tuning mine for years and does the one in the pub as well."

"Excellent," Lottie looked out of the window where she saw a small patch of blue sky amongst the grey, "but I think we'll not go down to the village until after lunch because hopefully it should have brightened up by then."

Early in the evening, Kate, on her way to the kitchenette walked through the room in the Old Bakehouse that at one time would have been the baker's shop. As she passed the door she saw five envelopes lying on the doormat. Surprised by the amount of post and the lateness of its delivery she leaned forward to pick the envelopes up but then instinct caused her to hesitate. Two of the envelopes were face-down and when she looked closer she observed that the three face-up could not have been delivered by the postman because there was no address written on the envelopes nor were there any stamps. On looking closer still she saw that the names on the envelopes were not written in ink but were made up with individual letters cut from magazines or newspapers. Feeling a tinge of excitement and realising the envelopes should not be touched she went into the kitchenette and took a pair of rubber gloves from the drawer. She then lifted the envelopes from the mat and laid them down on the dining table. She was puzzled; none of the envelopes were for occupants of the Old Bakehouse but were for – Norman Williams, John Hewitt, Jeff Barnes, Jim Bray, and Harry and Barry. Confused she gathered up the envelopes, took them into the living room and spread them out on the coffee table.

"Early Christmas cards?" Bill chuckled.

Kate shook her head. "I don't know what they are. It doesn't make sense because none of them are for us."

Sandra stood up and reached down for one of the envelopes.

"No, don't touch," shrieked Kate, "the police might want to examine them for fingerprints."

"What," laughed Bill, "why would the police want to see them?"

"Come and see," said Sandra, "then you'll know."

Bill scratched his head. "They appear to all be for the people who are in for a share of Joe's legacy but why leave them here?"

"And why are the names in cuttings from newspapers and stuff," questioned Zac.

"Spooky," giggled Vicki.

"Shall we open one?" Sandra asked.

Kate shook her head. "No, I don't think we should because they're clearly not for any of us. I think we ought to get Norman round here. Do you have his number, Dad?"

"It just so happens, I do. We exchanged numbers when Norman came back the other day."

Bill rang Norman who was in his hotel room having just taken a shower; he was at the door of the Old Bakehouse in less than ten minutes.

"I don't like the look of this," he muttered on seeing the envelopes.

Kate handed him the rubber gloves. "Put these on before you open yours."

Norman's hands shook as he tore open the envelope. Inside was a single sheet of paper. On it was a message also in letters cut from a magazine and newspapers.

Bill sat down on the arm of the sofa. "Read it out to us, Norm."

"There's not much to read, it simply says: *Sling your hook, guys. Greed is one of the 7 deadly sins. If you stay you will be punished.*"

Vicki laughed.

Sandra didn't think it was funny. "I'm ringing the police."

But Bill beat her to it and already had the number of the local police typed into his phone.

In due course two officers arrived and thanked the family for not having touched the envelopes without wearing gloves.

"I think we'll deliver these to their intended recipients to see if they contain the same message," said the older of the two police officers, "and then we'll take it from there."

"But who on earth is John Hewitt?" Vicki asked.

"I assume it should say Jack Hewitt," said Sandra, "and the person who sent it has simply got the name wrong. Jack is Irene's husband."

"Likewise they've spelled Geoff's name as Jeff," laughed Bill, "and written Barry and Harry when it should be Larry and Harry. It also looks like the sender didn't know the twin's surname."

"So whoever sent them clearly isn't very familiar with the set up," concluded Sandra, "and because they dropped them all here it looks like they don't know where they're all staying either."

"Or is that the impression they want to give," reasoned Kate, "and in reality they know very well who everyone is and where to find them."

Norman re-read his note again. "It's a pity they didn't drop mine off at the hotel because if they had they'd have been spotted on CCTV."

"Which is probably why they were left here," tutted Bill, "meaning whoever sent them obviously isn't daft."

Because the police officers insisted on taking away all of the envelopes for forensics to look at, Bill asked if he might be permitted to take a picture of Norman's message on his phone. The officers agreed and so after they left and drove away, Bill promptly rang the ladies at Primrose Cottage to tell them the latest news.

Hetty and Lottie knocked on the door of the Old Bakehouse in less than five minutes after Bill rang them. To save time they had arrived by car both having agreed that to walk would have taken far too long and wasted valuable time. After they had heard how Kate found the envelopes on the doormat and had read the message sent to Norman on Bill's phone, they sat down on the settee, brows knitted and lost in thought.

"I don't know what to say. Whatever can this mean?" Hetty was clearly miffed by the situation.

"Well, that's what I'm expecting you to find out," Bill's tongue was firmly in cheek, "I mean, why else would I have rung you?"

Hetty cast Bill an admonishing look as she peered over the top of her reading glasses.

"Well, for a start we can rule out Jim," Lottie concluded.

"Why?" Sandra asked.

"Because he calls everyone guys."

Hetty removed her reading glasses and returned them to their case. "That's a good point, Lottie."

Bill nodded. "It is because if it were him he would never address people that way as it would be a sure way of identifying himself."

"So," said Kate, "it looks as though someone is now trying to frame Jim for sending the messages the same as they framed Irene for the attempted murder."

"Good point," pondered Sandra, "So, I wonder, does this let Irene off the hook? I mean, she couldn't have sent the messages, could she? Because she's locked up."

"Sadly I fear it won't make any difference because it doesn't mean she didn't attack Biddy, does it? Even though we know she didn't." Hetty hoped her statement made sense.

Lottie groaned. "This is getting a bit too intense for me. One mystery is bad enough but three is really pushing my poor old brain cells."

"Three?" Norman queried.

Lottie nodded. "Yes, the attempted murder of Biddy, the body in the oven and now the messages."

Sandra sat down on the arm of the sofa. "Well, I don't think there's any question as to who put Geraldine's body in the oven. It was clearly Joe. Sorry, Norman, I know he was your father and all that."

"Please don't apologise because as much as it goes against the grain, I have to agree."

Hetty stood up. "My thoughts entirely and you're right, Lottie, there are problems to solve and for that reason I suggest we go and see Jack and Martha without delay to see what they have to say."

"Whoa, hold on there," laughed Bill, "at least give the police a chance to visit them first or they won't know what you're talking about."

Hetty sat back down. "Yes, you're quite right. I'm too impetuous and always have been."

"I think you ought to leave it 'til tomorrow, after all it's gone seven now and I know I don't like it when people knock on our door after dark." Sandra shuddered at the thought.

"Hmm, I must admit I don't either," conceded Hetty, "so we'll go to the pub instead and see if anyone there has any updates."

"Now that sounds a very good idea," Bill agreed, "Fancy a pint, Norman?"

"Yep, always got room for a pint."

"And what about me?" Sandra was indignant.

"Well, you can tag along if you want."

"Tag along!" Bill ducked to avoid the cushion that hurtled in his direction.

"Quiet in here tonight," observed Hetty, as she walked into the Crown and Anchor with Lottie, Sandra, Bill and Norman.

Bill looked at his watch. "Well, it's still quite early so I daresay it'll be busier later."

After Bill bought a round of drinks, he and Norman sat down on bar stools. Hetty, Lottie and Sandra who preferred to have something to lean on sat on chairs at a table quite near to the bar.

"There's Jim and Pamela," Lottie spotted mother and son sitting near the piano where they appeared to be finishing a meal, "I wonder if they've had a visit from the police yet."

"Only one way to find out," Seeing that Jim had laid down both knife and fork on his empty plate, Hetty beckoned him over.

"Ah, and that reminds me," Lottie waved her hand towards the piano, "Daisy rang just before you did Bill, and her husband is coming to tune the pianos tomorrow. Sorry I didn't mention it earlier but with this latest development it had completely slipped my mind."

"Mine too," admitted Hetty.

"Excellent. What's his name?" Sandra removed her scarf and gloves.

"Eric," said Lottie, "We've met him on a few occasions and he's a really nice chap."

Clutching a glass of beer, Jim approached the table where the ladies sat. "Hi guys, has something happened?"

"In a way, yes." When Hetty told him of the notes he looked shocked.

"Wow! Well, we've not had a visit from the old Bill yet but then I suppose they'd go to our home address if they didn't know we're staying at Tuzzy-Muzzy. Having said that they probably don't know our home address either."

"They would have gone to Tuzzy-Muzzy," Lottie assured him, "because we told them you were staying there but as you're in here I suppose you'll have missed them."

Hairdressers, Nicki and Karen who were sitting at the next table heard what was said and turned round. "Sorry for being nosy but what time did you find the envelopes?" Karen asked.

"I don't know," said Hetty, "because I wasn't there. What time was it, Bill?"

"Well Kate found them a little after six. I remember that because the news had just begun. I don't think they could have been there long though because they certainly weren't there when I got home from work and that was about ten past five."

"Why do you ask, Karen?" Hetty was curious.

"Because there was someone lurking around outside the Old Bakehouse when we locked up the hairdressing salon this evening."

"And they behaved in suspicious manner," added Nicki, "We both commented on it."

"In what way?" Norman asked.

"Well, the bloke pulled up the hood of his top when he saw us and scuttled off really quickly."

"He," questioned Hetty, "Are you sure it was a man?"

Nicki frowned. "Well, no I'm not but I assume it was a bloke because he had short hair, wore a baseball cap and a hooded top but on reflection it could just as easily have been a woman, I suppose."

"And to be fair the hair could have been long and tucked in the top so it would look short at a glance," Karen added.

"Did you see the colour of his or her hair and how tall do you reckon he or she was?" Hetty asked.

"We only got a glimpse because as I said, when he saw us he quickly pulled up the hood of his top over his cap and ran off. I'd say the hair was light but then again it's difficult to say because most of it was covered with the baseball cap," Nicki looked at Karen, "How tall would you say he was?"

Karen shrugged her shoulders. "Impossible to say but at a guess I reckon no more than five eight, if that."

"So it could have been a woman."

"Yes, I suppose so, but whoever they moved pretty quickly because they were out of sight in minutes."

"A woman with light hair so it's not the same person who attacked Biddy then," reflected Bill.

"It might be because Nicki only thinks his hair was light, so it might be the same person. Especially as it would have been dark by then." Lottie tried to visualise the person in question.

"Yes, it was dark and the nearest street lamp is several yards away so don't take my word for it because I'd never be able to swear his hair was light, dark or whatever in a court of law, it all happened so quick."

On a high stool at the bar sat Douglas Bell who listened carefully to what was being said. Before the subject was changed he joined in.

"Sorry to butt in but I've couldn't help but hear what you've been saying. You see, a few days ago, well, actually it was a Wednesday because I was at the church to give the old bells a tinkle and it wasn't this week it was last. Anyway, that night as I was walking up the church path I saw someone who fits the description you've just given lurking behind one of the gravestones. He didn't see me because he seemed to have his eyes transfixed on something or other out towards the street but I've no idea what."

"Perhaps he was hiding from someone," Karen suggested.

Douglas nodded. "Hmm, good point, he might have been."

"But who would he be hiding from and why?" Lottie tried to think.

"More to the point who is this person?" Hetty asked.

"Could have been a child playing hide and seek," Norman suggested.

Douglas screwed up his face. "I don't think it was a child. A teenager maybe but not a child."

"And I'm not even sure youngsters play things like hide and seek nowadays," sighed Lottie, "Not with all the electronic gadgets and stuff."

Norman chuckled. "He's probably a peeping Tom and was watching some lady in her boudoir. Which house is opposite the church?"

"Sea View Cottage would be the nearest," answered Lottie.

Norman's face dropped. "You mean where Irene and Martha are staying?"

"Oh, my goodness, yes," Lottie gasped.

Hetty opened her mouth to comment but closed it as her eyes were drawn to Douglas' feet. He was wearing flashy white trainers with blue squiggles down the sides.

"So do you think Douglas made up the story of someone being in the churchyard so we'd not suspect him?" Lottie was trying to make sense of Hetty's observation of which she had learned as they left the pub.

"Could be. I mean we know very little about him. He has longish dark hair and no doubt some light coloured tops. Although I have to admit most people probably have light coloured tops in their wardrobe."

"Yes, even I have but none of my tops have hoods."

Hetty laughed. "Good, we can rule you out then."

They crossed the road and began to walk up Long Lane.

"But seriously, if it was Douglas who attacked Biddy, what would have been his motive? He has nothing to do with Joe's will or anything like that as far as I can see."

"True." Hetty stepped aside to avoid treading in a puddle.

"And if it was him you saw that night it stands to reason he wouldn't have spoken because he hardly knows you?"

Hetty nodded. "Yes, you're quite right and so for now we'll just assume it was him I saw but that he's completely innocent."

Lottie frowned. "But then if it was him why didn't he go the police when they asked the squiggly shoe person to come forward and be eliminated from the enquiry?"

"Perhaps he didn't see or hear anything about it," reasoned Hetty, "I really don't know."

"Okay, so for now we'll give him the benefit of the doubt but keep an eye on him all the same."

"Yes, and we'll keep an eye on Pamela as well."

Chapter Nineteen

Inside the Old Bakehouse on Saturday morning, Daisy's husband, Eric was busily tuning Hetty's old piano which she was looking forward to playing again once it was installed at Primrose Cottage. The job didn't take long for its tuning was not far out, unlike the other which he anticipated would be hopelessly out of tune if it had not been played since Eve left in 1958. Once the task was finished, Sandra rang Basil who had previously offered to move the piano in his van.

"If you don't mind I'll come back and do the other one on Monday," said Eric, "because it could be another hour or so before Basil's been and taken this one away and I can't start the other because there's not enough room."

"Yes, I'm sorry about that. We should have moved it before you got here. Bill and Zac put one in front of the other to give me room to decorate and we've never bothered to separate them. They're both working at the moment and I don't think I could move it."

"No, you mustn't and it'd be unwise for me to try as well," admitted Eric, "I pulled a muscle in my back the other day and I don't want to make it any worse. But not to worry, I'm happy to come back another day."

"Are you sure? Of course sod's law, normally Basil would be here doing the kitchen but he tries to avoid working on a Saturday if he can."

"I don't blame him. Everyone needs time to themselves and Basil's a good worker."

"Yes, he is. He's been a godsend. I don't know what we'd have done without him."

Eric picked up his jacket.

Sandra felt a pang of guilt. "Are you really sure you don't mind coming back?"

"It's no trouble at all, Mrs Burton. I'm only ten minutes away and it's good to have a reason to come out for a stroll."

"Thank you, so much."

"Oh, and tell Hetty if moving hers puts it out of tune again I'll pop along to Primrose Cottage and fix it."

Shortly after Eric left there was a knock on the door. It was Ginny.

"I've had a word with everyone involved with Joe's will and we've all agreed that if you're serious about giving Crumpet a home then this would be the best place for him. Norman did show an interest, but said if it was possible, he'd rather Crumpet stayed in the village."

Sandra squealed with delight. "When can we have him?"

"Today, if you like. He's at the shop now with Alex."

"Well, I'll need to get a bed for him and stuff like that, then we'll be ready."

"No need," said Ginny, "you can have the bed he has at the shop, along with a lead, doggie bags, bowls, plenty of dog food and some toys."

"Gosh, thank you. So may I collect him now? Then he'll be here for when the girls get home from school."

"Of course, there's no time like the present."

On Saturday morning, volunteers from the village with the aid of a borrowed cherry picker were busy stringing up Christmas lights between telegraph poles and lamp posts. While outside the Crown and Anchor, Ashley Rowe the landlord helped unload from the back of a lorry a ten foot tall Christmas tree which was destined to stand on the corner of the pub by the car park.

Meanwhile, along the main street, Kate and Vicki proudly took it in turns to hold the lead of the newest member of the Burton family as they took him for a walk.

On Saturday evening, Harry and Larry, the builders from Penzance arrived at the Crown and Anchor. Sid saw them as they walked into the bar and beckoned them over to the table where he sat with Bill and Norman.

"Any news?" Sid asked.

Larry sat down while his brother went to the bar for drinks. "Yes we've had the tests done and got the results this morning. To our amazement they're positive."

"That's good news," said Bill.

"Well, it is and it isn't because it's made us feel a bit melancholy. I mean, after all these years of wondering about our parentage we now know who our dad was but it's too late to meet him. Having said that he probably wouldn't have wanted to see us anyway but we could still have looked at him from afar, couldn't we? If you see what I mean."

Sid tutted. "Yes, that is rough, mate, but if it's any consolation this chap here is also Joe's son and he didn't know that 'til a few weeks back. It wasn't through the will that he found out though but we won't go down that road because it's rather a long story."

"It certainly is," Bill agreed.

"And of course it means that Norman here is your half-brother." Sid patted Norman on the shoulder as a way of introduction.

Larry reached across and shook Norman's hand. "Pleased to meet you, brother."

"Not only am I your half-brother but Lucky Jim is as well. And we also have two half-sisters, Biddy Barnes and Irene Hewitt."

"Yeah, so we've been told and I believe one is in hospital recovering from a brutal attack and the other is locked up for attacking her."

"True, but there aren't many people who believe Irene, the one who's locked up, is guilty," insisted Bill, "ourselves included and we all hope that the police will come round to our way of thinking before long."

"Yes, and with any luck they'll dig a bit deeper now they've seen the notes that were sent out." The tone of Norman's voice indicated he did not really believe what he stated.

Larry laughed. "Ah, yes, the notes: they were most peculiar but I reckon they were sent by some moron who thought it'd be funny. I must admit they made us laugh."

Norman chuckled. "I'm inclined to agree."

"Anyway, don't forget you're in for a few thousand pounds' share of Joe's legacy," Bill reminded him, "so that should help mend a few wounds from the past."

"Yes, but we didn't really come here in search of money," said Larry, his expression doleful. "We were more interested in trying to find out who our father was. We've quite a profitable little business going so we make a good living. Looking for Dad was a wild shot and as it is, it's paid off in more ways than one. I just wish we'd looked sooner."

Meanwhile, inside the little-used dining room at Primrose Cottage, Hetty happily played the piano and didn't stop until her fingers ached.

"I hope you don't find my playing annoying," she said to Lottie as she returned to the sitting room and warmed her hands by the fire. "Please say if it does."

"Far from it, Het. I find listening to you play very relaxing and getting your old piano back was one of the best things we've ever done."

Hetty sat down on the sofa and put her feet on a footstool. "Good, that's music to my ears if you'll excuse the pun."

On Monday morning, Eric arrived bright and early to tune the other piano and to his surprise he found Hetty and Lottie at the Old Bakehouse drinking coffee in the sitting room with Sandra.

"Hive of activity here today," he commented on hearing the sound of an electric drill.

"Yes, that's Basil and Mark in the kitchen," Sandra acknowledged, "By the end of the day all the units should be in place. It's very exciting."

"And the carpet is being put down in here tomorrow so you better put your skates on, Eric," chided Hetty.

"We'll have less of your cheek, Hetty Tonkins. I do a thorough job and it'll be done in an hour or two as long as you don't start nagging."

"I'm pulling your leg, you muppet. Anyway, we're looking forward to the entertainment, aren't we, Lottie? It's been a while since I've seen a piano tuned."

"Well, before I start you can get off your backside and make me a coffee," chuckled Eric, "providing that's okay with Mrs Burton here."

"Of course but please call me Sandra."

After drinking his coffee Eric lifted the lid on the top of the piano and peered inside. "Hmm, as I thought there's a fair bit of muck in there. I think I'd better clean it out before I start tuning."

Intrigued as to how dirty it was Hetty also looked inside. "Cobwebs, and some of them look ancient too. Rather you than me, Eric as there might be one or two eight legged beasties still in residence."

"Yes, or I might even find a dead mouse. It wouldn't be the first time."

"I hope you didn't find one in mine," Hetty looked aghast.

"No, yours was as clean as a whistle."

"Ah, good, and might I be permitted to say you did a splendid job tuning it. It's never sounded better."

Eric took a bow and then continued with his work; when he was satisfied that the top part was clean he knelt down between the piano legs and fiddled with a catch beneath the keys. He was then able to remove the panel from behind the foot pedals.

"Hello, hello, hello what have we here?"

Intrigued by the tone of Eric's voice, Lottie, Hetty and Sandra all jumped up to see what he had found. Covered in dust was a parcel wrapped in a faded sheet of Christmas paper. He passed it to Sandra who blew off the dust and then carefully tore the paper apart. Inside were a brown patent leather handbag and a pair of brown patent leather, high heeled shoes.

"Surely that must be Geraldine Glover's missing bag and shoes," gasped Lottie, "Whatever are they doing in the piano?"

"Goodness only knows," Sandra picked up one of the shoes, "but Geraldine certainly had good taste."

"What's in the bag?" Hetty was eager to see.

"Only one way to find out." Sandra unfastened the strong handbag clip and tipped out the contents onto the floor. Eric watched with interest. Amongst the items was a purse, a hand mirror, lipstick, face powder, cake mascara, a door key, a Family Allowance book bearing the name Mrs Geraldine Glover, a lace edged handkerchief and a folded piece of paper bearing a recipe for bread pudding written on it by hand.

Hetty picked up the purse. "Old money," she sighed, taking out two one pound notes. The change she tipped into her lap. "It's so much heavier than the stuff we have today. It makes me feel quite wistful."

Sandra opened up the Family Allowance book. "Eight shillings a week. How much is that in today's money?"

"Forty pence," chuckled Hetty.

"I wonder why Joe stuffed these items in the piano instead of in the oven with Geraldine," mused Sandra.

"Perhaps there wasn't enough room," suggested Hetty, "after all Geraldine would have been a lot bulkier in the eiderdown back then than she was when we found her."

"But they wouldn't take up that much room," reasoned Lottie, "especially the shoes. I mean, why didn't he leave them on her feet?"

Hetty tipped the coins back in the purse. "Goodness only knows but I'm glad they've turned up because now we'll be able to pass them on to Irene. Well, we will when she gets released."

"*If* she ever gets released," sighed Lottie.

On Monday afternoon, Eve's ashes were buried in an area of the churchyard set aside for the deceased who had chosen cremation. The service taken by Vicar Sam was brief and attended only by Norman, Hetty, Lottie, Kitty and Sandra. Bill tried to get the afternoon off work but was unable to do so because several people were off sick.

"I thought Alice would be here," said Lottie, as they left the churchyard where a lone raven watched from the bare brown mound of earth beneath which Joe Williams lay.

Norman wiped a tear from his eye. "Yes, I thought she might like to join us as well but when I mentioned it she went very quiet and then cried. I think the fact that she and Mother spent so many years apart has really hit home. She said she'd come and visit the grave another time though. I got the impression it's something she'd like to do on her own."

Hetty tutted. "Yes, I can understand that. Families should never fall out or fail to keep in touch."

"And nor should friends," said Kitty, emphatically.

Chapter Twenty

Inside the Old Bakehouse on Tuesday Morning, Sandra patiently waited for the carpet fitters to arrive before she took Crumpet out for a walk. Meanwhile, just down the road in his room at the Pentrillick Hotel, Norman was painstakingly going through the boxes given to him by Sandra and Bill containing his late father's belongings. The paintings he had already looked through and told Bill and Sandra they could keep them all except for the seagulls on the beach which he wanted to hang in his Dawlish home. After looking at each item in the boxes he put them into one of four piles: items he wanted to keep, things that might interest his Aunt Alice, useful but unwanted items for the charity shop and things he considered of no use or interest to anyone. Amongst the articles he kept were a few toys and baby clothes which he assumed he might once have worn. There was also a baby's rattle, a lock of hair in an envelope and a book of baby's first achievements. His name was inside the book and Norman smiled to learn his first tooth came through when he was three months old and that he had taken his first step when he was ten months old. He sighed, baffled as to why his mother had not taken the book with her when she left but on reflection he liked to think that she had not done so, so that Joe would have something to remember his little son by. The son he would never see again.

"It doesn't have any bearing on Biddy's assault or the mysterious messages but because of the handbag and shoes I lay awake in the night thinking about the murder of Geraldine Glover," said Hetty, as she dried the last of the breakfast dishes and tipped away the washing up water. "I wonder if we've jumped to the wrong conclusion regarding her murder and it wasn't Joe who put her body in the oven at all but someone else."

"But we've already been down that road," reasoned Lottie, "you, Debbie and I tried for ages to come up with someone else but all agreed in the end that realistically it could only ever have been Joe."

"No, but there is someone else who would have been in the position to have done it."

"Really! Who?"

Hetty dried her hands. "You'll see. Get your coat on, Lottie, we're going to ask someone a few questions."

"But we haven't lit the fire yet."

"We'll do it when we get back. We won't be long."

To Lottie's surprise, Hetty drove to Porthleven. "Surely you don't suspect Alice. I mean, I see no motive there whatsoever."

Hetty switched off the engine as they pulled up outside the small cottage. "No, I don't suspect Alice but I think she might know more than she's prepared to admit."

When Alice answered the door she seemed pleased to see them. "Come in, come in. I made a cake yesterday and was going to freeze half of it because it'd probably be stale before I'd finished it but now you can help me eat it instead."

"That will be very nice, thank you," said Lottie.

With mugs of coffee in hand and slices of fruit cake on plates on laps the three ladies sat by the fire and commented on the dull, dark, damp days that seemed inevitable in November.

"We saw a picture of you the other day taken at the school when you were just five years old," said Lottie, after observation of the weather came to an end.

"Oh, was it amongst Joe's things?"

"No, it was in an album belonging to Charlie Pascoe," said Hetty, "Do you remember him?"

"What Charlie Pascoe the builder? Yes I remember him." The sisters noticed the colour had drained from her face.

"He was a handsome lad," persisted Hetty.

"Yes, yes," mumbled Alice. "And is…is…he still alive then?"

Lottie placed her empty plate on the floor by her feet. "Yes, he's in the care home in Pentrillick. We've been to see him a couple of times now."

"We wondered if he remembered bricking up the oven in the Old Bakehouse you see," added Hetty.

Coffee splashed from Alice's mug onto her skirt. "And…and…did he?"

Hetty shook her head. "Sadly not."

"Well, I'm not surprised after all it was a long time ago," Alice was focussed on dabbing her skirt with a tissue and didn't look up. "And have there been any further developments as regards the body in the oven?"

"Other than of course we now know who the poor lady was, there haven't and that's why we're here," Hetty watched Alice over the rim of her coffee mug, "You see, I think it's possible that Eve might have known something about it, don't you?"

Alice gasped. "Why would you think that?"

"A hunch, and the fact we now know that Joe was the father of Geraldine's daughter. Meaning if Eve suspected that, it would have given her a motive for murder, wouldn't it?"

Lottie shook her head. "Don't be silly, Het. Eve left in January 1958 so she wasn't around when the oven was bricked up."

"Ah, but did she leave in January though? We only have Alice's word for that, don't we?"

Alice looked uncomfortable; she put down her mug on the hearth slate, fidgeted and kept glancing towards the sideboard.

"Okay, I'll come clean but you have to believe me that when I first met you I really didn't know what happened back then but for some reason when you asked me when Eve left I felt compelled to lie. Probably because I knew deep down that she hadn't gone because she'd met someone else. She never went anywhere much, you see, so she couldn't have met someone unless he'd have been a regular in the shop but back then most of the shoppers were housewives so I thought that was unlikely. And having taken these things into consideration I thought there had to be another reason for her to have left and I was right. I suppose you'd call it instinct."

Alice stood up, threw the coffee stained tissue onto the fire crossed the room and took an envelope from a drawer of the sideboard. "I received this a couple of weeks back after your first visit but as you can see it was written almost a year ago. I can only assume that it must during that time have been lost in the post somewhere or other." She handed the envelope to Hetty, "Please read it."

"Are you sure?"

Alice nodded. "Yes, knowing that you've read it will probably relieve me of the burden I've suffered since it arrived. And when you read it you'll understand why."

"Read it out loud, Het," whispered Lottie.

Hetty took the letter from the envelope, unfolded it and read:

'November 21st 2017

Dear Alice,

I fear that my days are numbered and as I prepare to meet my maker I need to clear my conscience of a few things. I can't tell Norman, he would be horrified and so I must tell you.

Sometime in the future it's inevitable that Joe will die, the Bakehouse will be sold and the new owners will no doubt make changes to the property and I fear that one of the changes will be to expose or knock out the old oven. Should that happen then my guilty secret will be revealed.

You see, the reason I left Joe was not because I had met someone else. It was because I couldn't bear to live in the house knowing that Geraldine Glover was there too or should I say the remains of Geraldine. Please let me explain. I knew that Joe was unfaithful to me but had no proof and so one evening when he left home to go for a walk I followed him. Norman was asleep and I doubted I would be gone for long and I wasn't. Joe walked the short distance to St Mary's Avenue where he went inside Willow House without even knocking on the door. That was enough to confirm my fears. I knew Geraldine's husband was away at sea. If you remember he was an officer in the Royal Navy. For several days I kept my anger under control but of course said nothing to Joe. For some reason I didn't blame him. I blamed her.

A week later, Joe, after he'd done the baking, went off to Truro to visit his parents and left me to manage the shop. I remember it clearly, the weather was dry and sunny although a little chilly but then it was February. Norman was with you for the day. Do you remember? You took him to the beach wearing his new gumboots and he paddled in a rock pool. Bless him, he was just two years old. Anyway, I digress. While in the shop Geraldine came in wearing an obviously new two piece suit. It had a figure hugging jacket and a pencil skirt and she looked a million dollars. On her feet were a pair of brown patent leather high heeled shoes and she carried the patent leather handbag of which I'd always been envious. She seemed a little glum and was clearly disappointed to see me. I put it down to the fact her husband had returned home the previous day. And then she smiled sweetly and asked where Joe was in a provocative manner. She looked so glamorous standing there, beautifully made up and reeking of expensive scent while I, having had a *busy morning serving in the shop was all hot and bothered. Something snapped, Alice. I saw red, came out from behind the counter and told her to leave Joe alone. She laughed at me. I was furious and without thinking grabbed her by the throat. Despite her heels she was smaller than me. Less strong too. Before I realised what I was doing she lost her balance and fell away from my grip and onto the floor. As luck would have it, it was one o'clock and so time to close for lunch. I quickly locked the front door, pulled down the blind and dragged her into the baking room where I filled a glass with water and threw it onto her face hoping it would bring her round. It didn't work and to my horror I realised she was dead. Panic stricken I knew I had to dispose of the body so from the bottom of the wardrobe in the spare bedroom I took out an old eiderdown which had seen better days and wrapped Geraldine inside it. I then put her inside the old oven and pushed her right to the back. The reason I did this was because I knew Charlie Pascoe was coming the next day to brick up the oven and render the wall. The trouble was I didn't want him or Joe to see the eiderdown at the back and so I quickly filled two boxes with various odds and sods from around the house and inside the dustbin and then stood them in front of the eiderdown. I thanked God that the oven was huge.*

When he came home, I told Joe about the boxes and said it was to be a surprise should anyone expose the oven in the future. Joe thought it an excellent idea. However, to make sure he didn't pull the boxes out to see what was inside, I helped him with the baking the following morning and made sure he was not left in the room until after Charlie had arrived and started to brick it up. It was such a relief when the job was done and all evidence of Geraldine's visit to the shop was hidden away. Actually that's not quite true. I have to confess that I couldn't bear to see Geraldine's lovely handbag buried nor her matching shoes and so I kept them back to admire and pretend they were mine. Of course I couldn't let Joe see them and so I kept them hidden in the bottom of my piano.

The following day word got out that Geraldine was gone but to my relief her husband didn't seem bothered, in fact he almost seemed pleased and I even heard it said that he'd sent her packing. And so I thought I'd committed the perfect crime and was convinced I would never be found out. The trouble was my conscience got the better of me and as I said earlier, I couldn't stay knowing that Geraldine was there. And so in a way she probably won because she stayed in the house with Joe while I had to go away and leave behind everything I held dear except of course for Norman. I even lost Geraldine's shoes and handbag because in my haste to leave I forgot to pack them.

I hope, Alice that you will not think too ill of me. To tell you this has been a very difficult chore but I feel better already for having confessed to you. It's unlikely that I shall ever see you again...not in this life anyway. But thank you for the good times we had when we were children.

I hope you find it in your heart to forgive me.
Your sister, Eve.'

Hetty carefully folded the letter and returned it to its envelope. "Oh, dear, you poor soul. You must have been horrified when you received this."

"Yes, I was, and that's why I couldn't bring myself to attend the burial of Eve's ashes. I couldn't tell Norman why so just said it would be too upsetting. And of course knowing the letter had been lost for so long somehow made it all worse. It was like receiving it from a ghost."

"Have you told the police about the letter?" Lottie asked.

Alice shook her head. "No, I've told no-one. Do you think I ought?" Her voice was little more than a whisper, "I mean, it was so long ago."

"Yes," said Lottie, "you must if for no other reason than to clear Joe's name."

"But think of the affect it'll have on Norman. Surely it would be best to leave well alone. After all Eve's dead so she can't be brought to justice."

"I can't really see that Norman will be hurt any more than he already is," reasoned Hetty, "after all at the moment he thinks that his father was a murderer."

"But he doesn't remember his father, does he? In fact up until a couple of months ago he thought his father was Oscar Williams. He knew nothing of Joe."

"Yes, and I can understand where you're coming from," sympathised Hetty, "but I still think you should tell the police. After all it's not just Norman's feelings that are at stake. Remember he has half brothers and sisters who would be greatly relieved to hear that their father was innocent."

Alice slowly nodded. "Yes, yes, you're quite right. I promise I'll phone the police after you've gone although I'm not quite sure what to say."

"All you need do is to show them the letter," said Hetty, kindly, "It says all they need to know."

"And they'll be pleased because it will enable them to close the case," Lottie added.

As they rose and walked towards the door Alice asked, "Is the care home nice? You know, where Charlie is."

"Lovely," enthused Lottie, "very bright and with far reaching views of the sea. It's up behind the school."

"Yes, I know where it is although I've never been there as it wasn't built until after I'd left the village but my next door neighbour here worked there for a time. She's retired now and has moved away but the reason I mentioned it is because it's just come back to me that I remember her telling me and my husband about a scandal there donkey's years ago. It had no bearing on Eve of course but apparently one of the staff there sucked up to the wealthier residents whose memories were vague. She found fault with their grown-up children and sowed seeds of doubt as to their worthiness and then suggested they leave *her* some of their money in their wills. She slipped up though because one of her victims was more astute than she realised and when the victim's daughter next came to visit, her mother told what she suspected."

"Oh dear, so what happened to her?" Hetty asked, "The gold-digger, that is."

"She was instantly dismissed and as far as I know left the area."

"Sadly that sort of thing seems to happen quite a lot," said Lottie, as they walked into the hallway.

"Yes, I suppose it does. Anyway, if you go to the care home again, please tell Charlie I send my regards."

"We will," Lottie squeezed Alice's hand and then opened the front door.

As they climbed into the car Hetty glanced back at the cottage where Alice waved to them from the sitting room window. "I suppose we ought to have told her about the messages sent to Norman and the others even though we all think they're the work of a prankster."

Lottie closed the car door and fastened her seat belt. "Maybe, but I'm glad we didn't because I think she's got quite enough to think about without that. Poor Alice. It must have been difficult for her to come to terms with the fact her sister was a murderer, that's if she has yet, and I can quite understand why she lied to us as regards the date Eve left Pentrillick."

"So can I, and you're right about the messages because I daresay Norman will tell her as he's bound to pay her a visit before he goes back home."

Lottie sighed. "Yes, poor Norman I think he'll be devastated when he hears the truth about his mother."

Chapter Twenty-One

The following evening, Jackie arrived in the village and because all rooms at the Pentrillick Hotel were taken she attempted to book a room at Tuzzy-Muzzy. To her dismay, despite the fact it was November, she learned the guest house was fully booked too.

"I've seen you before, haven't I?" Chloe who ran the guest house asked.

"Yes, I was down a little while ago. I'm a friend and next door neighbour of Norman Williams. You know, the chap who is the son of Joe the baker. Well, one of them anyway."

"Ah, yes, of course. If you'll just hang on a minute I'll see if I can find you somewhere to stay."

Jackie sat down in the reception area beside a tall rubber plant while Chloe went into the office. When she came back out she was smiling. "I've found you a room and it's not far away. It's next door in fact with Lottie and Hetty. Lottie is the mother of Bill who along with his family have bought the Old Bakehouse. They have a single room which they'd be happy to let you have for as long as you want."

"Oh, I know who you mean. An elderly couple of sisters, twins I believe. I met them when I was here last time."

Chloe smiled. "That's right but I'd try and avoid referring to them as elderly if I were you especially when they're in earshot."

"Point taken."

"Anyway, if you go round now you'll find they're waiting for you. You can't miss it. It's the house next door and it's called Primrose Cottage. You'll see the name on the gate."

"Brilliant. Thanks…err…"
"Chloe, I'm Chloe."
"Yeah, thanks, Chloe."

"So," said Hetty, later that evening as she walked down Long Lane with her sister and Jackie, "you didn't book a room at the hotel because you wanted to surprise Norman and when you got here and found it was full up you went to Tuzzy-Muzzy on their recommendation?"

"That's right, I never dreamt the hotel would be full at this time of the year and again I can't thank you enough for helping me out. At one point I thought I'd have to go home which would have been dreadful because I've taken a week's holiday especially to be here."

"No problem at all," said Lottie, "it's nice to have some young company."

"So out of curiosity, can you tell us what Eve was like?" Hetty asked, "We don't like to bother Norman and it'd be nice to get a picture of her from someone who wasn't a family member anyway."

"Of course," Jackie's face broke into a smile, "Well, apart from the fact she was tall, slim and elegant, what else would you like to know?"

"Well, how long had you known her and stuff like that?" Hetty was careful not to be indiscreet.

"I see. Well, Mum, Dad and me moved next door to Eve and Norman several years ago and not long after Eve's husband, Oscar had died so of course we never knew him. Actually, I should correct that, shouldn't I? After all we now know that Eve and Oscar weren't married. Anyway, Mum and Dad liked Norman and Eve and so they often spent time with each other. You know, Mum would pop in for coffee with Eve and they'd come to us for a drink on Christmas morning and stuff like that.

At the time I had a boyfriend and we'd been going out together for a couple of years and then one day he met someone else and dumped me. I was heartbroken."

"What a cad," blurted Hetty.

Jackie laughed. "I would have agreed with you back then but to be honest I'm glad we're no longer together."

"That's alright then," said Lottie, "please continue."

"Well, after Liam left I was at a bit of a loose end and so one day I popped in to see Eve knowing that she was on her own because Norman was at work."

"Sorry to interrupt but where does Norman work? We've never actually asked him," said Hetty.

"He's something to do with insurance but I'm not quite sure what."

"And what do you do?"

"I'm a waitress-cum-barmaid so I work irregular hours."

"I see."

"Anyway, when I went to see Eve she could see that I was upset so asked me why and I told her all about Liam. She was so sympathetic, bless her and I have to admit it made me cry. After that we became good friends and I often popped in for a chat, but sadly not long after that her memory started to go and she was eventually diagnosed with Alzheimer's. Norman was distraught and so knowing she loved music and playing the piano, he bought some karaoke equipment hoping that if she was able to sing it might help her overcome her memory loss. We had some wonderful times together; Eve had a gorgeous voice and between us we learned how to sing 'Bohemian Rhapsody'. You know, as in Freddie Mercury and Queen."

Both sisters nodded.

"Anyway, gradually she got worse and Mum and I took it in turns to help Norman look after her. I was with her on the morning before she died. It was strange, the room seemed eerily quiet and Eve appeared to be sleeping and then suddenly she opened her eyes and reached out for my hand. "I've done some bad things in my life, Jackie," she said, "Do you think God will forgive me?" I told her that he would and she seemed to be content after that. She died a few hours later. I remember looking at the clock. It was one o'clock. Mum and I were with her and so was Norman."

As they reached the bottom of Long Lane, Hetty and Lottie noticed in the light from the street lamp that there were tears in Jackie's eyes. She paused before they crossed the road. "I suppose one of the bad things she considered herself to have done would have been leaving Joe the baker and taking Norman away but that's not such a bad crime, is it? I mean, you often hear of families breaking up."

Hetty felt her cheeks flush. "When did you last speak to Norman?"

"Oh gosh, it must be several days ago now. It might even be a week."

"So you've not heard of the latest developments?"

"Norman told me about the messages but he reckons it was a prank. Is there something other than that then?"

"Yes, but let's get inside by the fire and then we'll tell you."

With Hetty and Lottie dreading the revelation they must disclose, the three ladies crossed the road and went into the Crown and Anchor.

Inside Primrose Cottage the following day, Lottie was seated by the fire watching the early evening news; Jackie had gone into the village to see Norman, and Hetty was in the kitchen preparing their dinner. As Hetty strained hot vegetable water from the saucepan into a jug and stirred in gravy granules she thought about Jackie and the misery she and Lottie had caused her when they had told her that it was Eve who had taken the life of Geraldine Glover and not Joe. Her mind then drifted back to their recent visit to see Alice and she wondered how the elderly lady had fared telling the police of her sister's ghastly crime. And then there was the conversation they'd had with Alice when leaving her cottage in Porthleven as regards the person who had tried to trick residents at the care home into leaving her their wealth.

Hetty stopped stirring. Pamela had worked at the care home in the nineteen sixties and left abruptly. She insinuated that she'd left of her own free will. Was that the truth or had she actually been sacked? Was she the woman of whom Alice had spoken? Hetty dished up the dinners with haste and carried the hot plates into the sitting room to share her thoughts with Lottie.

The following morning, the sisters walked down to the village and knocked on the door of 4, Main Street. Natalie Burleigh, still wearing her dressing gown, answered.

"Oh no, we haven't dragged you out of bed have we?"

"I was up but only just. I was on duty last night and should have finished at midnight but then one of the carers had to go home because she was feeling unwell and so I stayed on until four this morning."

"That's so thoughtless of us," said Hetty, "we do apologise."

"Not a problem. Would you like to come on in?" She stepped back so they could enter the small passageway and waved her hand towards the living room.

"I'll put the kettle on because I'm dying for a cup of tea. Would you ladies like one too?"

"That would be lovely, thank you," said Lottie. Hetty agreed.

"So do you have some exciting news?" Natalie asked after the tea was made.

"Not very exciting and more of a question really," acknowledged Lottie.

"I'm intrigued. Fire away."

Hetty took a sip of tea and then placed her mug on the coffee table. "We went to see Alice yesterday. I don't suppose you know her but she's the younger sister of Eve. Eve being Joe the baker's second wife."

"I know who you mean. I've heard Norman speak of her." Natalie sat down on the arm of a fireside chair.

Hetty nodded. "Yes, of course. Anyway, as we were leaving she told us about someone who worked at your care home back in the nineteen sixties who was dishonest. Apparently this woman used to make a big fuss of wealthiest residents with poor memories and then try and persuade them to leave her some money when they popped their clogs. Have you heard anything about that?"

Natalie shook her head. "No, I haven't but then I've not been there long."

"Do you think you could find something out about it?"

"I could try although I'm pretty sure there's no-one around now that's been there anywhere near that long but they still might know of something. May I ask why you want to know?"

"Of course, of course," said Hetty, "but promise you won't tell anyone?"

Natalie giggled. "That sounds sinister but don't worry I'll not say a word to incriminate you."

"It's to do with old Joe's inheritance and the people who are likely to benefit from it. It seems someone is trying to upset the applecart, so to speak. First Biddy was attacked and then there were the weird messages..."

"...But we think they were done by a prankster," Lottie reminded her sister.

"Yes, yes, we do. The thing is we're wondering if the person who was grooming the old folks back in the sixties might be Pamela Bray. We know she worked in the care home back then because she told us she did. What's more, she seems determined to get hold of some of Joe's money."

"Is the Pamela you're referring to, Jim Bray's mum?"

"Yes, but of course she wouldn't have been a Bray back then because that's her married name," Lottie pointed out.

"How fascinating, I wonder if it was her. I'll ask around tomorrow when I'm back at work and let you know one way or the other. I must admit I'm probably as intrigued as you are"

"Thank you," said Hetty, "we appreciate that."

Lottie nodded. "And now we must leave you to get dressed otherwise the day will have gone."

"Sadly it will. I'm not too keen on these dark dull days before Christmas."

"Me neither," Hetty agreed; "roll on spring."

"Oh, I've just remembered," Natalie stood as the sisters prepared to leave, "Your daughter-in-law asked me the other day if there were any job vacancies at the care home and there are. Two in fact both part-time so if she's still interested get her to call this number and ask for Diane. She's ever so nice and I know for a fact that she prefers to have people working there who live in the village." Natalie wrote the number down on the back of a used raffle ticket.

"That's good timing," laughed Lottie, "because we're going along there now to see the kitchen which is finished at last."

When they arrived at the Old Bakehouse, Lottie repeated what Natalie had told her and gave Sandra the piece of paper.

"So we assume you're thinking of working at the care home," said Hetty, "Do you think you'd like it?"

"I'm sure I would. I mean, I know some of the jobs will be a bit grotty but I've got a strong stomach so can handle that." She tucked the piece of paper in her pocket, "I'll give this Diane a ring in a minute while I make the tea. Anyway, come and see the kitchen. I think you'll be impressed."

The sisters followed Sandra through the kitchenette and then into the transformed baking room.

"Oh, my goodness, it's gorgeous," gasped Hetty, "and the oven door has come up really well."

"It has, hasn't it? Bill rubbed it down and painted it with a special paint. He's very proud of it."

Hetty opened the black oven door, peeped inside and then shuddered.

"So what will you do with the kitchenette?" Lottie asked, "I mean, it's surplus to requirements now you have this lovely room."

"Bill and I were discussing that last night and we're not sure. I mean, we could knock out the wall between it and the dining room to make that much bigger or we could have the sink, cupboards and so forth removed and then use it as a sort of office or just a spare room. What do you think?"

"Not sure," confessed Lottie, "I mean, knocking down the wall would make an awful lot of dust which seems a shame when you've just got the place ship-shape. What do you think, Het?"

"I'm inclined to agree and the dining room is more than big enough for the five of you."

"Yes, it is but we were just thinking about Christmas and things like that when we'd need more table space. Having said that there's enough room for ten people already so I suppose we'll forget that idea for now and we can always do it in the future anyway."

"Did you get the carpet in the sitting room done alright?" Lottie suddenly remembered that it was due to be fitted on the Tuesday just gone.

"Yes, we did and we love it. Come and see. We're thrilled to bits now the room is finally done."

The sisters followed Sandra into the sitting room where Bill who had the day off work was sitting on the couch. He stood as they entered the room.

"Wow!" Lottie was awe-stuck, "What a transformation. It doesn't look like the same room as when you first moved here."

Hetty slipped off her shoe to feel how soft the carpet felt. "Hmm pure luxury and it goes beautifully with your furniture."

"Thank you," said Sandra, "we think so too."

Lottie looked at the wall between the two front windows. "I see you've hung up Joe's painting of the robin. That's a lovely touch."

"Ah, but look what we've given pride of place to," Bill waved his hand towards the wall above the piano.

"The raven," gasped Lottie.

"No," chortled Bill, "it's a scruffy crow."

On Friday evening, Hetty and Lottie went to the Crown and Anchor where they had planned to meet up with Debbie. The sisters arrived first and to their delight found their favourite table near to the fire was free. When Debbie arrived they were surprised to see she was accompanied by her husband, Gideon.

"Lovely to see you, Gideon," said Hetty, as he and his wife sat beside each other on the opposite side of the table to the sisters, "and I see you're having a drink."

Gideon smiled. "It's only lager shandy so I'm playing safe. As you know I'm no drinker."

Debbie took a sip from her large glass of wine. "I insisted he come out with me because it makes me feel guilty when I leave him at home."

"Well, you shouldn't feel guilty, love. I go out and leave you when I play the organ at church and when I go to work."

"Yes, but you only work a couple of days a week and it's not the same as being left in the evening, is it?"

"Whatever you say, dear. Anyway, if you'll excuse me I see Sam's here so I'll go and have a word with him and leave you ladies to talk about women's stuff."

"Women's stuff," chuntered Hetty, as Gideon crossed the bar towards Vicar Sam.

Lottie smiled. "Yes, but to be fair he's quite right, isn't he, Het?"

"I suppose so." As Hetty reached for her glass of wine, her phone beeped. Hurriedly she pulled it from her handbag and saw she had a text message from Natalie. As she read it her face dropped.

"Oh, well, back to the drawing board. Natalie has asked around at the care home but no-one it seems knows anything about the woman in question." Hetty returned the phone to her handbag.

"There must be another way to find out," reasoned Lottie, "I mean, the sixties isn't that long ago, is it?"

Hetty laughed. "It might not seem it to us but it's actually fifty years ago and more so a lot of folks around here weren't even born then."

"No, I suppose you're right which makes me feel quite old."

"Have you tried Googling it?" Debbie asked, "Because quite often if you type in the right keywords it'll pick up something or other. I mean, I daresay it got into the local papers at that time so something might come up about it."

"Good point," Hetty took out her phone again, "What shall I put?"

"What's the care home called?" Debbie asked.

Lottie shook her head. "No idea."

Hetty switched on her phone. "Me neither."

"Hmm, in that case go for a few keywords like Pentrillick, Pamela, care home, residents and financial exploitation and see if that picks anything up." As Debbie spoke she was aware that someone was behind her. She turned to see Pamela Bray, her face was a ghostly white and tears filled her eyes. "I can't believe you think it was me," she whispered.

Hetty's jaw dropped. Lottie's cheeks glowed red. Debbie fiddled with her hands.

"We…it's just…well…" Hetty muttered.

"It's just we heard the other day about the business at the care home in the sixties and you told us you were there then and so we..." Lottie couldn't continue.

"...Put two and two together and made five." Pamela sat down heavily on the chair vacated by Gideon.

Hetty's face was nearly as red as the poinsettia on the ledge behind her. "A lot more than five."

"So, do you know who she was?" Debbie nervously asked, "The woman at the care home, I mean."

Pamela nodded. "Yes, her name was Freda George and she was a nasty piece of work. I daresay she's long dead because she was in her late forties back then and a heavy smoker too."

"May we get you a drink?" Lottie forced a smile.

"Yes, please. Vodka and Coke." Pamela remained glum.

Lottie took her purse from her handbag. "I'm so sorry for, well, you know."

"So am I," mumbled Hetty.

Debbie nodded. "Me too."

As Lottie went to the bar Hetty fiddled with a beer mat. "Please let me explain, Pamela. You see, well, we're just trying to find out who attacked Biddy because we're sure it wasn't Irene and we want to get her released so when we heard about the care home thing and the fact someone there had been dishonest we thought we'd better check it out because we knew you'd worked there and ... I'm so sorry."

"It's okay, I can see where you're coming from and I'm pretty thick-skinned. In fact if I were in your shoes I'd probably have thought the same. What's more I'm on your side because I think Irene is innocent too and so does Jim." Pamela's look was still stony but then lips quivered and her face broke into her huge grin. She leaned her elbows on the table and looked at Hetty and Debbie in turn. "So," she said, "if I'm not the bad guy, who is?"

Chapter Twenty-Two

On Saturday December the first, Hetty woke early and looked from her bedroom window. The morning was dull and a fresh wind was blowing from the south west. The deadline for applications for a share of Joe's legacy had ended at midnight and she prayed that all those eligible for the windfall were safe and well.

Likewise, next door inside the single room he occupied at Tuzzy-Muzzy, Jim Bray woke up and looked at his phone. He noted the date and heaved a sigh of relief; there had been no threats to his life and soon he would be able to collect his cheque and return home to normality. With a huge grin on his face he leapt from his bed and with a spring in his step went into the en suite bathroom for a shower; he then went downstairs to the dining room where he met his mother, Pamela for breakfast; she was equally jubilant.

Meanwhile in Penzance, builders, Larry and Harry prepared for another day's work; they usually took Saturday off but because there had been a lot of rain during the month of November they were a little behind with their schedule and keen to catch up.

At the Pentrillick Hotel, Geoff Barnes ate an early breakfast for he was eager to get to the hospital in Truro to pick up his wife, Biddy, who was well enough to leave.

In the same hotel, Norman was woken by his phone ringing.

"Congratulations," said a familiar voice, "looks like you and your siblings are in for a six way split."

"Jackie, I thought it'd be you."

"So will we be celebrating later? After all the Christmas lights go on tonight so there should be a lovely atmosphere."

"Yes there should and I'd love to celebrate but it doesn't seem right somehow, not with poor Irene still being locked up. On a brighter note though, Biddy's on the mend and is being released from hospital today."

"Is she?"

"Yes, I saw Geoff when I got in last night. He'd not long been back from the hospital."

"Oh, that's brilliant then. But as you say the Irene factor does rather put a damper on things. I just wish the police weren't so convinced she's guilty but then we can't really blame them because the evidence does seem to be stacked up against her."

"Yes, it does and I've just remembered something else, Jackie. When I got in last night, Anna, one of the receptionists here said that a single room will be vacant as from today if you're interested."

"Oh wow lovely, tell her yes please. I mean I've enjoyed my few days here with Hetty and Lottie but I'd rather be independent as you well know. It'll be nice to be back in the village too and nearer the pub."

"That's what I thought. I'll book the room for you then when I go down for breakfast."

Inside Sea View Cottage there were no signs of jubilation. At the table in the kitchen, Jack and Martha sat and unenthusiastically ate slices of buttered toast.

"I suppose Mum's new found siblings will be rejoicing today," said Martha gloomily.

"Don't be bitter, sweetheart, they've all had their problems and to be fair to them they're all on our side."

"I know, but Mum's had it far worse than the others and she's still suffering."

Jack reached across the table and squeezed his daughter's hand. "Have faith, Martha. I'm sure something will crop up soon to prove your mother's innocent."

"Humph! Not while that dumb Inspector Fox is in charge. As far as he's concerned there's no need to even look for anyone else."

"You don't know that for certain."

"I do. I was here when he arrested Mum and it was horrible."

Inside his office, Detective Inspector Fox went through the evidence and statements regarding the assault on Bridget Barnes for a third time in as many days. The evidence against Irene Hewitt seemed pretty conclusive yet he wasn't convinced and Bridget herself refused to believe that it was Irene who had attacked her despite the fact she fitted the description given and held the accused's necklace in her hand. Furthermore, Irene wasn't in need of money so the motive was thin and it *was* feasible, as many people claimed that she had been framed, but if that were the case, by whom? Was it possible someone had broken into Sea View Cottage and stolen the necklace? Possible, yes, but there was no evidence to back it up. Then there were the envelopes containing notes sent to the persons due to benefit from the will of Joseph Williams. Who was behind that childish hoax and did it matter? He thought it unlikely and already the incident had been marked and dismissed as the work of a prankster, hence to pursue said person further would be a waste of police time and resources.

He re-read the statement by Henrietta Tonkins who claimed that she saw a figure near to the alleyway leading down to the beach shortly before she found Biddy unconscious. Henrietta, or Hetty as she insisted she be called, swore blind that the person was not Irene but regrettably had been unable to give a description, due to having her head bowed against the inclement weather, other than to specify the person in question wore flashy white trainers with blue squiggles down the sides. As a result of that identification they had put out a request on the radio and in local newspapers for said person to come forward so that he or she might be eliminated from the enquiry but to date had received no response. Was it possible then that the mystery person seen by Hetty had just attacked Bridget Barnes? Possibly, on the other hand it was most likely someone who didn't live in the area and so was unaware of the police request.

Detective Inspector Fox gathered up the papers and returned them to their file.

"Something will turn up, I'm sure. I feel it in my bones."

"Can we get a Christmas tree today?" Vicki asked, as the family sat round the table eating breakfast in the dining room at the Old Bakehouse, "after all it is December now."

Sandra frowned. "I thought we'd decided to have a real one this year."

"We did," said Vicki.

"Well in that case it's too early as it'll have no needles left on it by the twenty fifth." Bill sprinkled brown sugar on his porridge.

Vicki scowled. "But hundreds of people are selling them on roadsides and other places and have been for some time now so people must be buying them."

"Well, perhaps they like vacuuming up pine needles," teased Sandra, "but I don't. Besides, we have a new carpet in the sitting room and so I don't want it messed up in the first month of having it."

"You could put an old rug under the pot," reasoned Vicki, "or even a sheet of polythene."

"Maybe but it wouldn't prevent the needles falling, would it?"

"Some trees have needles that don't drop so readily." Kate was keen to back up her sister.

"Yes, and they're a lot more expensive," Bill replied, "and I think we've spent quite enough lately."

Sandra nodded. "We certainly have."

"Well I think it's not fair," persisted Vicki, "one of the girls in our class at school said her tree went up a week ago. What's more, the Christmas lights get switched on in the village tonight so if we don't have a tree we'll look like real party poopers."

Sandra shook her head. "I intend the tree to go in between the two windows which means it won't be visible from outside anyway so no-one will know whether we have a tree or not."

Vicki's answer was not verbal; the sulky expression on her face conveyed her feelings perfectly.

Remembering how much she loved Christmas when she was sixteen Sandra felt a sudden pang of guilt. "Okay, I'll give you a choice. If you want a tree up today it'll have to be our old fake one which is currently in the outhouse but if you want a real one you'll have to wait for at least another week. I think that's fair, don't you?"

"Very," Bill stood and pushed back his chair, "Meanwhile I must get to work as it's bound to be another busy day in the supermarket."

As a compromise it was finally decided to put up the artificial tree in the dining room and then a week later to have a real tree for the sitting room; the girls were happy with that and so spent the morning dressing the tree which they stood on an upturned box and placed near to the dining room window.

At lunch time, as Sandra and the three children ate omelettes, Zac's phone beeped.

"Message from Em," he said, "she's offered to take me up to Pentrillick House to visit the Christmas Wonderland this afternoon and wonders if you girls would like to go too."

"Yes, please," gushed Kate, "then I can do a bit of Christmas shopping."

Vicki agreed.

Sandra reached for her handbag and gave the girls each a twenty pound note. "You'll love it. It's really Christmassy. I went up the other day with Grandma and Auntie Hetty while you were at school."

Amongst the items purchased by Vicki was a large bunch of mistletoe.

"Where are you going to put that?" Kate giggled.

"You'll see."

When they arrived home Vicki hung the mistletoe from a hook over the front door.

Kate frowned. "That's a daft place to put it unless you're hoping to steal a kiss from the postman."

Vicki looked smug. "Well I was thinking that maybe the vicar might call on his parishioners over the festive season."

In the evening it seemed the entire village was out to see the Christmas lights switched on. Among the large group of people which included members of the church choir were Hetty, Lottie and their family and friends; they all assembled outside the Pentrillick Hotel and then walked along the main street towards the Crown and Anchor, singing Christmas carols. When they reached the pub, Vicar Sam said a few words and then switched on the lights which were greeted by a chorus of oohs and aahs from the delighted crowd.

Afterwards many people went into the pub where waitresses handed out complimentary mince pies and glasses of mulled wine. Zac worked at the bar alongside Tess, Alison and Ashley. There was not a seat to be had and there was very little room for standing.

In the games area, Kyle was playing pool with Douglas watched by Kate, Vicki and Emma.

"Ding Dong Douglas is quite good," Kate watched in awe as he potted three balls in succession.

Vicki sighed. "Yes, he is. Pity he's not female."

As she spoke, Jackie passed by on her way back from the Ladies and heard what was said. "Anyone fancy giving me a game of pool?"

"Yeah, probably one of Zac's sisters," chortled Kyle.

Jackie looked at the twins. "Are you good players then?"

Kate laughed. "No way, we're rubbish."

"Oh," Jackie turned towards the lads. "So which one of you is the best player?"

Kyle pointed to Douglas and Douglas pointed to Kyle.

Jackie shook her head. "Which one do you reckon is the best?" She asked Emma.

"Tricky one but I reckon Kyle has the edge and he is the team captain."

"Really! Right, Captain Kyle, I'll give you a game then." Jackie selected a cue from the rack.

"You're on." As Kyle prepared the balls he suddenly felt nervous for there was a smug expression on Jackie's face and he noticed the twins edging their stools nearer to the table. Kyle's apprehension was justified; Jackie was a champion player in her home town and when play began she potted all the balls without Kyle getting a look in. The twins watched open mouthed. Kyle and Douglas were both speechless.

"Can't you come and live down here?" Vicki asked, "If you did you'd be able to teach us girls how to play and then we could thrash the boys."

"You could teach the boys how to play as well," laughed Kyle, who was still in shock.

Jackie smiled sweetly. "I'd love to live here, I really would but it's not that easy, is it? I mean, where would I stay and work?"

"You can get lodgings with Norman," suggested Kate.

"But Norman lives in Dawlish, next door to me and my parents in fact."

"I know," said Kate, "but I heard him talking to Mum and Dad while the lights were being switched on and he said he's seriously thinking of moving back down here seeing as this is where he was born and stuff like that."

"So are you serious about moving down here?" Bill asked Norman, "or were you just momentarily moved by the twinkly lights and the carols, especially 'Silent Night'?"

"I'm serious. I mean my roots are here and then there's Aunt Alice. It appears she has no family, just me and so I ought to be here for when she gets older. After all she is Mum's little sister and I'd make up for all the lost years," He smiled, "and Mum's here too now so I'd like to be able to look after her grave even if it's tiny and in time I'd like to get a memorial stone for her."

"Well if you do decide to make the move at least you'll know several people here and I for one would be delighted if you did."

"I'll second that," agreed Sandra, "We feel close to you because of your connection with the Old Bakehouse."

"Thank you, that means a lot. When I get home I'll look into it and do my sums. I've been with the same firm since I was a lad so I reckon I could easily take early retirement. And to be honest I'd welcome that but I don't want to say too much yet and raise Aunt Alice's hopes."

After the initial rush the pub gradually quietened down and when Bill went to the bar for a round of drinks he commented on the amazing turnout.

"Yes, it's always like this on lights switching on nights," said Alison, "Next thing will be all the Christmas parties for various firms and organisations and between you and me I'm not looking forward to that as at present we could do with a few more waitresses."

"Really! Would sixteen year olds be of any use?"

Alison smiled. "If you mean your twins then they'd be ideal. I mean they're well-mannered and if they're as efficient as Zac they'd be most welcome."

"I'll mention it to them then. It's about time they did a bit of work for their living."

"Well if they're interested send them round in the morning. If they come at the same time as Zac we can have a chat before we open up."

"Well," sighed Lottie, when they arrived back at Primrose Cottage, "tonight sort of made up for all the bad things that have happened of late. I must admit I thoroughly enjoyed it."

"Me too and I don't know about you but I think a nice cup of cocoa is in order and then bed."

"Lottie stood up. "I'll make it since you made lunch today."

As Lottie left the room Hetty glanced towards the sideboard where Geraldine Glover's patent leather shoes were tucked beneath and her handbag stood on top waiting for the day when they could be passed on to her daughter, Irene. They had thought of giving them to Martha but decided that reminders of her grandmother's plight on top of her mother's might be insensitive.

For some unknown reason Hetty felt the urge to look again at the contents of the handbag and so picked it up and tipped everything onto the coffee table. Again the old money made her feel nostalgic but handling someone's personal belongings brought on a feeling of sadness.

Hearing Lottie close the microwave door, Hetty quickly prepared to return the items to the bag; as she did so her fingers felt an unidentified object tucked beneath the lining. She looked for a hole where something might have slipped but the seams were all intact. To examine the lining further she put on her reading glasses and looked again at the seams. Down one side the stiches had clearly been sown by hand. Hetty took a pair of nail scissors from her own handbag and carefully snipped at the stitches. Inside the lining was a small card. A Christmas card with a robin and a heart shaped holly wreath on the front. Hetty opened it up. Inside was a small black and white photograph of Joe along with a simple message. *To the love of my life. A union forbidden now but perhaps in another world we'll be together forever. Happy Christmas my darling, Geraldine. Love and kisses always, Joe. xxxxxxx*

Chapter Twenty-Three

On Sunday morning after church, Kitty informed Hetty and Lottie that the police case regarding the death of Geraldine Glover was closed and so in the afternoon following a trip into Helston for groceries, the sisters took a detour through Porthleven on the way home for they were keen to see Norman's Aunt Alice to make sure that she was well and not feeling depressed having blackened her sister's name. They found her outside her cottage, standing on a chair, singing 'Deck the Hall with Boughs of Holly' as she cleaned the downstairs windows.

"Oh, hello," she said, as they opened her gate and stepped onto her garden path.

"We've just been into Helston," Hetty informed her, "and thought we'd pop in to see you while we had the car out to make sure you're okay. I hope it's not inconvenient."

Alice jumped down from the chair. "No, not at all. It's always nice to have visitors as I don't get out as much since my husband died."

Alice picked up the chair and carried it into her kitchen. Hetty and Lottie followed.

"Tea?" Alice asked.

"Only if you you're having one," said Lottie.

"Well, actually that was my intention. I told myself I couldn't have a cuppa until I'd cleaned the downstairs windows. So I thought I better do it."

After the tea was made they all filed into the small sitting room where Hetty and Lottie sat on the couch and Alice sat in her favourite fireside chair.

"We're very proud of you for telling the police about Eve," said Hetty, "It was a courageous thing to have done and it's enabled them to close the case."

"Yes, maybe. It's certainly eased my conscience. Anyway, say no more about Eve's doings and tell me instead, is there any more news about the attempt on that poor lady's life?"

"Sadly not," conceded Hetty, "the police are convinced Irene Hewitt did it and have charged her so they won't be looking for anyone else."

"Well, from what Norman's told me the evidence against her seems pretty strong and so I can't say that I blame them."

Hetty shook her head. "No, I mean yes, we agree about the damning evidence but at the same time we think there's more to it than that. It's just too simple. What's more we really liked Irene."

"Her husband and daughter are very nice too," Lottie added, "and they're both terribly upset."

"I don't doubt Irene is a nice person: after all we now know that she is definitely Joe's daughter and as I've said before, I liked Joe."

"What about Geraldine Glover, Irene's mother? Did you know her at all? If she died in 1958 you would have been eighteen then."

"You're quite right, I was eighteen and I did know her. That's to say I knew who she was and I daresay we'd have passed the time of day had we met in the street but she was quite a bit older than me and so there was nothing to unite us."

"No, I suppose not."

"Have you seen Norman lately?" Hetty suddenly asked.

"Yes, he was here a couple of days ago. Why?"

"Did he tell you about the messages sent to all the people who should receive money from Joe's estate?"

Alice smiled. "Yes, he did. What do you make of it?"

"Well, having given it a lot of thought I'm inclined to believe it was someone in the village who did it for a joke," Hetty admitted.

Lottie nodded. "I agree and I think the police do too."

"Really! You don't think it was one of the party trying to frighten off the others then?"

"Well, if it was," laughed Hetty, "it didn't work because they're all still here having stayed to reach the deadline."

"Hmm, I suppose you're right."

"Which of course was at midnight the night before last, so hopefully now everything will return to normal." Hetty finished her tea and put the empty mug on the floor.

"So how many people came forward hoping for a share of Joe's money?" Alice asked.

Hetty shrugged her shoulders. "We don't know for sure but rumour has it that dozens took the DNA test and many were negative so it looks like it'll be a clean six way split."

"Six!" spluttered Alice, "How can it be that many? I'm sure Norman only mentioned five."

"No, definitely six," Lottie counted on her fingers, "There's Norman of course and then Biddy Barnes, Irene Hewitt, Jim Bray and the twins Larry and Harry whose surnames I can't remember."

"Me neither," Hetty added.

Alice sniffed. "Ah, yes, the twins of course. For some reason I'd counted them as one."

After chatting for an hour or more the sisters said they ought to be getting back as it would soon be dark and they had left washing on the line.

"Do you mind if I use your loo before we go?" Hetty asked, as she stood and stretched her arms, "Having had a cup of tea I might be cutting it a bit fine if I wait 'til we get home."

Alice laughed. "You have my sympathy, dear. The bathroom's upstairs second door on the left."

"Thank you, I'll be back in a jiffy."

Before Hetty went into the bathroom, she paused outside the first door on the left. It was slightly ajar and so she peeked into the room. It was neat, tidy, very quaint and obviously Alice's bedroom. Next to it was the bathroom and the only other door was closed. Determined to peek in there too, Hetty tiptoed across the landing and opened the door. To her horror it squeaked. Nevertheless, hopeful that Alice and Lottie were still chatting and so had not heard she peeked around the door. Against the opposite wall was a dressing table and a large mirror. Make-up lay in trays on the surface of the table along with several pairs of spectacles. A pair of dark coloured trousers and a light jacket were draped over the back of a chair and on a shelf several dummy heads were donned with wigs in varying shades and styles. Hetty chuckled to herself as she went into the bathroom. "Looks like Alice likes to go out in disguise sometimes." As she flushed the toilet, the penny dropped. Hetty quickly washed her hands; as she reached for the towel she saw a pair of flashy white trainers with blue squiggles on the side tucked beneath a stool. With her heart in her mouth she descended the stairs and cautiously opened the sitting room door. She froze. Alice stood behind the couch where Lottie sat, her hands and feet bound with sticky tape. A large kitchen knife lay on the back of the couch and in her hands Alice firmly held the two ends of Lottie's scarf.

"You had to have a look, didn't you?" Alice's once gentle voice was now aggressive. "I knew you were nosy the moment I first set eyes on you."

"We heard the door squeak, Het."

"Shut up." Alice pulled the ends of the scarf tighter round Lottie's neck.

"But...but *you* can't have tried to kill Biddy. I mean, you're seventy eight so much too old."

Alice threw back her head and laughed. "Old I may be but unfit I am not. You see, when I realised we couldn't have children I took up running. I've run dozens of marathons over the years and have the heart of someone fifty years my junior." She looked at the door, "So don't bother running away because I'll catch you if you do."

"But, but why did you do it?" Hetty asked.

"Isn't it obvious?" Alice hissed, "That money belongs to Norman. Okay, I know Bridget, Biddy or whatever she calls herself was his firstborn but Joe gave her away. He didn't want her. And as for Geraldine's girl, Joe didn't even know she was his. I reasoned by getting shot of Bridget I could get rid of Irene as well. Two for the price of one. Pretty good going I reckon."

"Humph," grunted Hetty, "But you seem to have forgotten that Biddy is on the mend and because Irene is innocent she'll soon be released. I happen to believe in British justice."

"Well more fool you," cackled Alice, "The evidence against her is pretty rock solid. It's a pity they did away with hanging though. As for Biddy perhaps I'll try again. I'd like to dispose of Barry and Harry too but I saw them the other day and they look big strong lads so I suppose they'll have to stay."

"Larry and Harry not Barry and Harry," corrected Lottie.

"Yes, and then there's Jim Bray," Hetty reminded her.

Alice shuddered. "I'm not messing with him either. I've seen his mother, she's a whopper."

From inside Hetty's handbag sounded the ring tone of her mobile phone. Her eyes darted towards it.

"Leave it." Alice picked up the knife.

"But if I don't answer it whoever is ringing might be concerned."

"No, they'll think it's not a convenient time for you to answer which of course it isn't." Alice laughed.

"But..."

"Come and sit down here beside your sister or my hands might slip." She put the knife between her teeth and pulled the scarf tighter round Lottie's neck as if to prove she wasn't bluffing. Hetty sat down and clasped her sister's taped hands. Alice stepped out from behind the couch, picked up the sticky tape and knelt in order to wind it around Hetty's wrists. The knife she placed on the floor by her feet. "Put your hands together as though in prayer and hold them out in front of you."

Fearing for her sister's life, Hetty did as she was ordered. When both sisters were bound, Alice stood up.

"What do you intend to do with us?" It was Lottie who spoke.

Alice picked up her mobile phone from a foot stool and proceeded to send someone a text message. "You're both going for a swim." She put down the phone and from a cupboard took several plastic carrier bags. "But before that I need you to wear these bags on your heads."

"But we'll suffocate." Hetty was aghast.

"That's the general idea," laughed Alice, "but don't worry, I'll make a better job of it this time because there's no rush. I can't believe that damn woman survived. Still, practise makes perfect."

"You're bonkers. You'll never get away with it."

"Oh yes I will." She unwound the scarf from Lottie's neck, "You don't need this anymore."

Lottie rubbed her throat with her bound hands to relieve the pain.

"So let me get this right," said Hetty, her eyes fixed on the knife back in Alice's hand, "You plan to suffocate us with those bags and then chuck us in the sea."

"No, don't be silly," scoffed Alice, "the sea's too difficult to reach from here and I don't really like walking over sand and shingle anyway especially if it's wet."

Hetty was confused. "So where are we going for a swim as you so cruelly put it?"

"The boating lake in Helston. We'll go after dark when there's nobody about." She looked at the cuckoo clock, "What time does Lidl close?"

"What! Are you planning to go shopping after you've disposed of us?"

"Of course not. I just want to know what time it closes so I know when there will be no-one there."

"Four," whispered Lottie.

"Four! Don't be daft they don't close that early."

"They do on a Sunday," snapped Hetty.

"Of course, yes, it's Sunday, that's perfect then because they should be locking up and going home very soon. I didn't really want a late night so I might as well get things moving as soon as possible." Alice laid down the knife and hummed as she sorted through the carrier bags, "

"One more question," said Hetty, playing for time, "How on earth do you propose to carry two corpses out to your car? We'll be dead weights."

Alice laughed and shook her finger at Hetty. "Dead weights. I like it."

"I wasn't being funny and you haven't answered my question."

"You can't go in my car because I don't drive."

Hetty felt a glimmer of hope. "So how will you get us to the boating lake?"

"My accomplice will help me."

"Your accomplice!" Hetty's glimmer of hope vanished.

Lottie tried to keep calm. "And who might she be?"

"He," snapped Alice, "my accomplice is a man."

Hetty gasped as the chance of escape lessened.

Lottie, however, was keen to know more. "So who is this man?"

"My son." Alice spoke with pride.

"Your son! But you said you couldn't have children." Hetty was confused.

"No, I didn't."

"Yes you did," said the sisters in unison.

Alice shook her head. "No, I said *we* couldn't have children, not *I*. It was my husband who was infertile."

As she spoke they heard a car pull up outside and a door slam followed by loud footsteps running up the garden path. Whoever the footsteps belonged to then opened the front door and entered the house without knocking.

"What's wrong, Auntie?" Norman was breathless as he ran into the room. He stopped dead when he saw the sisters bound in sticky tape. "Hetty, Lottie. What on earth's going on?"

"They know I tried to kill Bridget, Biddy or whatever her name is so I need you to help me to dispose of them."

Norman's face turned white. "You did what?" He flopped down in the fireside chair.

"I tried to kill Bridget, Biddy or whatever her name is," Alice waved the knife as she repeated her claim, "I can't believe the damn woman survived."

Norman shook his head. "I don't believe you. I mean how? Why?"

"How? It was easy. After all I have lots of time on my hands and so I put it to good use and started going over to Pentrillick on a regular basis wearing all sorts of different disguises, not that anyone would have recognised me. I must admit it's been really handy having lots of wigs and clothes to choose from, all of which I've picked up in Helston's charity shops over the years but then I always have liked dressing up."

"But you don't drive," Norman interrupted, "so how did you get to Pentrillick?"

"On the bus of course. I used my bus pass."

"But if you were in disguise and used your bus pass surely the driver would have noticed you didn't look like your photo on the card," reasoned Lottie.

Alice tutted. "Don't be daft. As long as you look to be in your sixties or older they don't check. And if he had said anything I'd just say I'd dyed my hair. Now, where was I?"

"Going to Pentrillick on the bus," Hetty prompted.

"Ah, yes. Right, while in Pentrillick I watched to see what Irene and her daughter got up to. Surveillance I think they call it. You should try it, it's good fun. I watched from the churchyard to establish where they were staying and then went and hid in the back garden of their cottage. While there I saw them put the house key under a big flower pot. I was over the moon as it meant I'd be able to get inside the house and have a good poke round. So when I heard them drive off I went indoors and saw a necklace lying on a bedside cabinet. I knew it belonged to Irene because there was a picture of her mother, Geraldine, inside looking just as I remember her, so I took it. But I'm not a thief because I knew she'd get it back after Biddy was found."

"You broke into Sea View Cottage and had a good poke round!" Hetty gasped, "And you call me nosy."

"Well, don't stop there," said Norman, noting Alice appeared to have come to the end of her explanation, "what did you do next?"

"That's obvious, isn't it?"

"No."

"Humph! Of course it is. I waited for the opportunity to get Bridget alone and I knew it wouldn't be difficult because I'd been watching her, too, you see, and knew that she and her husband Jed or whatever he's called went to the pub most nights during which Biddy frequently went out for a fag."

"Biddy's husband isn't Jed, he's Geoff," corrected Lottie.

"Well whatever. I'm not very good at remembering names."

"So what happened?" Norman urged.

"After seeing their routine my plan was simple. It being, I'd follow them to the pub on my chosen night, wait for Biddy to come out for a fag and then strike. As it was I didn't have to wait that long because minutes after I got there to begin my surveillance outside the hotel, I saw her come out alone and go for a walk through the village where to my delight she took a stroll along the beach. It was getting dark and there was no-one about because it was a windy old night. When on the beach I quickly hid behind one of the boats and changed the blonde wig and baseball cap I was wearing for the dark curly wig. I then changed my dark blue hoodie for a light coloured jacket and popped on some glasses I own which are very similar to the ones Irene wears. In the jacket pocket was the necklace and all these I had in a carrier bag."

Alice's account was interrupted when the cuckoo emerged from behind his door and announced that it was four o'clock. She patiently waited until he was safely back inside before she continued.

"Right, where was I? Yes, I remember, I'd just changed my clothes. Anyway, after that I left the blonde wig, baseball cap and blue hoodie behind the boat and then walked along the beach with the now empty carrier bag. I then crept up behind Biddy and popped it over her head. It was a piece of cake because she's a right little squirt. Anyway, when she stopped struggling I pulled out Irene's necklace and forced it in her hand making sure it was wrapped round her fingers so it wouldn't get washed away when the tide reached her. I then changed back into the blonde wig, baseball cap, and blue hoodie and put the light jacket and accessories back in the carrier bag, left her on the beach and caught the bus home knowing if anyone had seen me from the windows in the buildings alongside the beach they would describe the attacker as being dark haired and wearing a light coat. To my delight the tide was coming in fast so I knew she was in for an imminent dip." She pointed to Hetty and Lottie, "Just like these two ladies here will be in an hour or two."

"But fortunately I found Biddy before the tide got her," said Hetty, smugly, "so your efforts didn't quite go to plan, did they?"

Alice turned red with rage. "So it was you found her! I might have known. You're such a busybody."

"Did you send the silly messages too?" Norman asked.

"Of course I did and they weren't silly."

"Humph! That's a matter of opinion," scoffed Hetty.

"They were silly, very silly and you're a hypocrite," said Lottie, "After all murder is one of the seven deadly sins as well as greed."

"Absolutely," chortled Hetty, "and a much more serious one too."

Alice dropped the knife on the floor, seized an empty vase which stood on the sideboard and quickly raised it over Hetty's head. Norman promptly sprang to his feet, grabbed the vase, tossed it into the fireside chair he had vacated, kicked the carrier bags away from his aunt and with trembling hands picked up the knife.

"Don't stab them," shouted Alice, her arms raised in horror, "it'll make a mess on the carpet."

Ignoring his aunt, Norman cut the sticky tape that bound the sisters' wrists and ankles and set them free. He then phoned the police.

Chapter Twenty-Four

It was after seven when Hetty and Lottie arrived home and so they had to bring in the washing by torchlight. While Lottie shook each item and placed it on the clothes horse, Hetty looked in the fridge for something to eat.

"I don't know about your thoughts, Lottie, but I don't seem to have much of an appetite at the moment. In fact I think a large glass of wine sounds a much better option. How about you?"

"I think that sounds a great idea but we'll have to go to the pub because we finished off the last bottle here a couple of days ago."

"Even better."

"And before we go I'll ring Bill and get him to meet us there. I'm sure he and Sandra would like to hear the full details of today's little adventure and best to hear it from us rather than a distorted rendition from someone else." Lottie picked up the clothes horse and took it into the sitting room where she placed it a safe distance from the log burning stove.

When they arrived at the Crown and Anchor they found all were eager to hear of the day's activities. Bill, Sandra and the twins were already there having been primed up by Lottie's phone call. Norman was not present but appeared soon after with Jackie; he looked forlorn. Zac was also in and playing pool with Luke Burleigh; Emma was watching and at the same time giving Natalie a brief outline of the day's events as learned from Zac.

"Come, come over here," Hetty rose from her seat and took Norman's hand, "you look in need of a few friends."

"I've got Jackie and she's a brick despite her young age."

Hetty stroked Jackie's hand. "Yes, of course."

"Can I get you both a drink?" Bill asked.

Norman nodded. "Thank you, that's very kind. A pint of Strongbow, please."

"And I'd like a lager," said Jackie.

"How are you feeling?" Lottie asked as Bill went to the bar.

"Confused, relieved, bewildered and even a little angry."

"Relieved," repeated Lottie, "why relieved?"

"Because now Irene will be freed and quite quickly I should imagine, so she'll be able to attend her mother's funeral on Wednesday without a police escort. I was dreading that."

"Of course. With all that's been going on I'd forgotten the funeral."

"And how is Alice?" Hetty was almost afraid to ask.

"She seems fine. When they took her away she was like a child. So different to how she'd behaved earlier. It was almost like witnessing the antics of a female version of Doctor Jekyll and Mr Hyde."

"I must admit I was surprised by her change of character too. She was so nice when we first got to her cottage and seemed genuinely pleased to see us." Hetty hesitated before she continued, "I don't know whether you can help, Norman, but there's something bothering me. You see, when she told us she had an accomplice who would help dispose of our bodies she referred to him as her son."

"Yes, she said the same thing to me the other day. I called her Auntie and she said I'm not your auntie I'm your mother. Poor soul I think she's muddled and put it down to the letter she received from Mum recently. It's all been too much for her."

"You've seen the letter then?"

"Oh, yes, she showed it to me after you and the police had seen it."

"So why did she refer to you as her son?" Lottie asked, "It doesn't make sense."

"It doesn't," From his pocket Norman took a sheet of paper and unfolded it. "This is my birth certificate. I have it with me because I intended to show it to Aunt Alice when next we met to put the records straight. See, it clearly states that my parents are Joseph Percival Williams and Evelyn Florence Williams." He handed the certificate to Hetty.

"So why would she say otherwise?"

Norman shrugged his shoulders. "As I said, I just think she was muddled. Something went haywire in her brain. Must be something like that for her to have tried to kill Biddy Barnes."

The following day Hetty was still puzzling over the relationship between Norman and Alice. "I'm going to pop along to the care home, Lottie. Would you like to come with me?"

"To visit Charlie?"

Hetty shook her head. "No, actually it's Nellie I want to see but we can see Charlie as well."

Lottie frowned. "You think Nellie might be able to shed some light on the day of Norman's birth then?"

"Yes, she seems the obvious person to ask."

When they arrived at the care home they were greeted by Natalie. "Charlie's in the residents' lounge sitting in his usual place."

"Well actually we'd like to see Nellie first if that's alright."

Natalie's shoulders slumped. "Okay but you mustn't stay long. She's in her room and not very well at the moment. One of the visitors yesterday evening carelessly told the residents about the arrest of Alice who several of them knew, Nellie included. For some reason she's taken it really bad and is too weak to get up."

Nellie turned her head towards the door as they knocked and then quietly entered her room; she attempted to smile as they walked towards her. "Have you come to see me?"

"Yes," said Hetty, "and we hear you're not feeling too good."

"No, I'm alright it's just well…never mind."

"It's a lovely morning," said Lottie, looking from Nellie's window which had a sea view.

"Yes, so Nat said. So what brings you to see me?"

"I'd like to be able to say it's just to see how you are but that would be dishonest because I have to confess that we, I, have an ulterior motive."

Nellie smiled. "That's sounds sinister. Pull up a couple of chairs."

Hetty and Lottie sat down one on either side of the single bed.

"You look very pale," Lottie commented.

"Well, I do feel a bit fragile but it's nothing to worry about." She attempted to sit up and so Hetty and Lottie each took one of her arms, adjusted the pillows and made her comfortable.

"That's better, thank you," Nellie smiled, "So what's the ulterior motive?"

"Well," Hetty slowly began, "I know all cases you've dealt with over the years are confidential but the well-being of a dear friend depends on what I need to ask you. Oh this is tricky, I'm trying to select my words with care but it's not easy."

Nellie leaned forwards and patted Hetty's hand. "I've a sneaky feeling I know what it is, dear."

"You do?"

"Would it by any chance be about a birth, many years ago in 1956?"

Hetty was taken back. "Yes."

"I wondered how long it'd be before it came to light. Because of all the goings on, I mean." She smiled, "It's been the talk of the place for a while. The body of poor Geraldine Glover being found in an oven; the attempted murder on the beach and then someone came to visit last night and told us the latest news."

Hetty nodded. "The latest news being Alice's arrest."

"Yes."

"So, what can you tell us? We don't want to confuse you." Lottie was afraid Nellie might pass out.

"You won't do that, dear. I may be frail and unsteady on my legs but my mind once I get into gear is as sharp as a needle. Anyway, I'll tell you what I know and to be honest it'll be a relief." Nellie leaned back in the pillows. "I was born in 1933 and so was just twenty three back in 1956."

"Yes, you're the same age as Charlie. He showed us a photo of you all back in your schooldays."

"That's right it's a lovely picture. My parents had a copy too and now I have it. Look," She pointed to a framed picture standing on a chest of drawers and smiled, "Strange isn't it? We were at school together and now we're both up here together," She paused and looked down at her hands, "I'm thinking how best to put this as I don't want to sound indelicate, if you see what I mean."

"No rush," said Lottie, kindly, "not after all these years."

"No, I suppose not. Anyway, Alice was fifteen when she discovered she was pregnant," blurted Nellie, "and her parents were furious, especially her father who was very strict. At first they thought about sending her away but then they came up with what they thought to be a better idea. You see, their older daughter, Eve had recently married Joe Williams, the baker and so they thought if the baby could be passed off as being born to Eve they'd have the best of both worlds. The family reputation would be saved and the baby born, who would of course be their grandchild, could be treated as such. However, to pull it off they needed the help of us midwives. My superior was told of the situation and was the only other person who knew what was going on other than me. To keep our silence, Alice's parents donated one hundred pounds to the village school and that was quite a bit of money back then. The plan worked well. I called in to see Alice regularly until we considered it was no longer possible to conceal the pregnancy. She then went away to a home up-country somewhere; a place where they took care of girls in her situation. Meanwhile, back in Pentrillick, Eve, with the aid of some padding, pretended to be an expectant mum and I called on her purely for show." Nellie smiled, "We'd drink tea during those visits, and talk about television and film stars while eating saffron buns made by Joe. Anyway, it worked. After the baby was born, Alice came home and Eve and Joe showed off the new baby boy. No-one ever doubted who his real mother was because there was no reason to question it." Nellie bit her lip, "I never breathed a word of what really happened to a soul. Alice saw quite a bit of her little boy as she helped look after him so that Eve could work in the shop. Then suddenly Eve left and took him with her and we never saw either of them again. Soon after Alice married and moved to Porthleven and I don't think for a moment her husband ever knew that she had a son."

Lottie frowned. "But what about the birth certificate? It clearly states that Joe and Eve were the parents."

"The baby's birth was registered by Cyril Johns who was Eve and Alice's father so he made sure it said what he wanted it to say."

"So Eve, who Norman believed to be his mother and the person who murdered Geraldine Glover, wasn't his mother at all."

Nellie shook her head. "No, she wasn't, Alice was and strictly speaking she still is."

"But he's still the son of someone guilty of attempted murder, isn't he, because his birth mother, Alice, tried to murder poor Biddy?" Lottie reasoned.

"Oh what a tangled web we weave when we practise to deceive," sighed Hetty.

Nellie smiled. "So true."

Lottie still looked puzzled. "I've one more question, Nellie, and you probably can't answer it anyway. But who was Norman's real father? Because it's just occurred to me that if it wasn't Joe then he'll not be entitled to a share of Joe's legacy."

Nellie smiled. "Oh, but he will be because the name of the father on the birth certificate is quite correct. Joe Williams was Norman's father. I don't know whether anyone else knew but Alice told me herself one day when I went to see her. She was a very attractive girl and was crazy about Joe even though he was twenty one years her senior but she had to keep her feelings under wrap. Of course Joe didn't feel the same way about Alice or Eve either if you ask me. In fact Eve herself told me that she married Joe to get away from her father and Joe married her so that he'd have someone to help run the business."

"So almost a marriage of convenience," said Lottie.

"Yes, I suppose it was but don't get me wrong I believe they were fond of each other but it wasn't love. There was only ever one true love in Joe's life."

"And who might that have been?" Hetty asked.

"Why Geraldine of course. She was a Trelease back then and Joe was besotted with her. They were childhood sweethearts, you see, but when they got older Geraldine's father put his foot down and forbade her to continue with their courtship. The Treleases were a well-to-do family, you see. They made their money in mining and thought themselves a cut above everyone else, especially Geraldine's father, who was a terrible snob. Poor Geraldine, if she couldn't marry Joe then she didn't want anyone."

"But she did marry," said Hetty.

"Yes, she did and that was because when war broke out, Joe joined up and met and married Cicely on the rebound. On hearing this Geraldine realised all was lost and so married someone or other Glover. I can't remember his name but he was a big noise in the Royal Navy. Fate is so cruel though because two days after Geraldine married Glover, Joe's wife died in childbirth and so he was footloose and fancy free again, until he married Eve some nine years later that is."

"Of course," whispered Hetty, remembering the Christmas card concealed inside the lining of Geraldine's handbag. "It all makes sense now. Because Joe and Geraldine's relationship was forbidden they continued to meet in secrecy even after she had married the Glover chappie and he had married Eve."

Nellie's eyes twinkled. "Yes, and in a funny sort of way I don't blame them."

Lottie glanced towards the school photograph taken in 1945. "So in a short space of time, Joe lost Geraldine, Eve and Norman. No wonder he closed the shop and never baked another loaf again."

Chapter Twenty-Five

The following afternoon, as the sun slowly sank behind the tower of St Mary's Church, Geraldine Glover was finally laid to rest and because Joe Williams was the last person to be buried in the graveyard it so happened that her final resting place was beside the man who she had loved long ago.

As Vicar Sam conducted the graveside service, watched on by a lone raven from the turrets of the church tower, Norman, his hand held tightly by Jackie, wept for the wrong done by the woman he thought to be his mother who had taken him from his father when just a small boy of two. Seeing his tears choked Irene and so after she had dropped petals onto her mother's coffin she too took his hand. "Please don't torture yourself, Norman. You're in no way to blame for what happened. It was a long time ago."

"That's what I keep telling him," whispered Jackie.

"But my moth…that woman Eve… was a murderer and she killed your poor mother." Norman sobbed as he looked down at Geraldine's coffin, "I think it's only just hit me. Until now I would have said she didn't have a bad bone in her body."

"Yes, but had it happened today it would be regarded as a crime of passion," said Irene, kindly, "We know it wasn't premeditated and my mother did appear to goad Eve as the letter sent to your Aunt Alice proved."

Norman sighed. "Aunt Alice! My real mother! Whatever's going to happen to her?"

"I think," said Irene's husband, Jack, "that she'll be treated leniently and her counsel will plead guilty with diminished responsibility. After all these have been the most extraordinary of circumstances."

"How can you both be so kind to me when it was my aunt...mother who framed you Irene for Biddy's assault?" Norman felt humble.

Irene stood on tip-toe and kissed his cheek. "Because I am innocent and I am now free. The misery and anger I felt is a thing of the past and my sympathy now lies with you, dear Norman...dear brother."

Slowly everyone left the churchyard and made their way to the Crown and Anchor where a lavish buffet was laid out in the dining room. Outside it was dusk and the glow of the fire was a welcome sight in the hearth of the village pub.

In the games area the youngsters were making the most of what little time they had with Jackie before she returned home to Dawlish. Nearby Vicar Sam was shaking hands with Irene Hewitt who he was pleased to see, although a little pale, was in relatively good spirits after her spell behind bars.

"Your vicar's a handsome bloke," remarked Jackie, as she watched him circulate amongst the mourners.

"Well if you come and live here you might be able to marry him," giggled Vicki, "We're seriously thinking about it ourselves but have to admit he might be a bit too old for us. Still we can always dream."

Vicki's comment caused Jackie to spill her drink. "I don't think I'm the sort of person a vicar would marry, do you?" She laughed at the notion.

"Why not?" Kate asked. "You're kind and jolly. You like people and people like you."

Jackie pointed to her spiky hair, the studs on her earlobes and the tattoos on her fingers. "Anyway," she said, "even if I did look the part I'd have competition because I reckon your vicar is rather taken with Martha Hewitt."

Near to the fire sat Biddy and Geoff Barnes. Biddy looked well considering her ordeal and her husband was very attentive. After Biddy had drained her glass of white wine she opened up her handbag and took out a packet of cigarettes.

"Oh no. You're not going outside in the cold surely?" Geoff scolded, "Not after what you've been through."

Biddy stood up and smiled. "No, Geoff, I'm not," she then crossed to the fire, threw the packet into the flames and returned to her seat. "I shall never smoke again and that's a promise. Having looked death in the face I now know the true value of life."

"It's weird, isn't it," said Irene, as she stood beside the table where sat Hetty and Lottie, "when I first arrived in Pentrillick I had no idea where my mother might have gone and nor did I know who my real father was and now the two lie side by side. I like to think they are happy with the way it's all turned out. I know I have peace of mind now."

Hetty smiled. "Yes, but isn't it sad that in years to come when we're all dead and gone that anyone wandering around the churchyard reading the tombstones will have no idea of the connection between Geraldine and Joe."

"No, but then some things are best left quiet."

"It's probably a silly thing to say but you were no doubt pleased to get your mother's handbag and shoes back?" Hetty had noticed at the funeral that Irene was holding her mother's bag.

"Oh, I was delighted, thank you, and I shall keep and treasure them always, except for the Christmas card, that is. I no longer have that in my possession because I asked that it be placed in Mother's coffin."

"Really?" Hetty was surprised, "I thought you'd want to keep that."

Irene shook her head. "I did for a while but then I realised it was never meant for my eyes and therefore wasn't something I felt entitled to keep. I took pictures of it inside and out beforehand though so I have something to remember it by. And I don't know whether you noticed when at the church but I had a heart shaped holly wreath made for Mum just like the one on the card."

As she spoke her husband Jack came up behind her and slipped his arm around her waist. "I've just been talking to young Jim. I think at the moment he's completely overwhelmed with everything."

Irene smiled. "I'm not surprised. A lot has happened in the last few weeks and to be honest it'll be nice to get home and back in a routine of some kind."

"So when do you go home?" Lottie asked.

"Tomorrow and in spite of what I just said I'll miss the village and especially its inhabitants. You've all been very kind."

Hetty looked out towards the sun terrace where through the steamed up glass doors Martha was just visible talking with Vicar Sam. "And I suppose Martha will be going home with you."

A broad grin swept across Irene's face. "Yes, she will but I daresay she'll be back on many occasions over the coming months and I like to think Sam will pop up to Bath too whenever he gets the chance."

"Are you suggesting there might be something between them?" Hetty optimistically asked.

Irene smiled. "It's not for me to say but I've never seen Martha's face light up as it does when she sees Sam."

Over by the piano, Bill and Sandra looked with interest at a framed map of Pentrillick, newly acquired by the licensees, and familiarised themselves with certain locations.

Bill put his arm around his wife's shoulder. "It's nice to be able to say this is a map of the village we can call home, isn't it?"

"Absolutely and I feel quite proud, especially as we live in one of the village's oldest buildings. What's more I think we've done pretty well in the few weeks we've been here. We've got the place done up, you've settled down in your new job, the girls are happy at school and look forward to earning some money waitressing and Zac starts his plumbing apprenticeship in January."

"And you might be going to work at the care home," Bill added, "Have you decided one way or another yet?"

Sandra nodded. "Yes, I think I'll definitely take the job. According to your mum and Auntie Het the residents are very nice and I've had a chat with Natalie and she really enjoys her work. What's more, Diane is lovely too so I'd have a nice boss."

"If you're at work though it means poor Crumpet will be left all alone."

"Well, the hours I work will be irregular but if it happens that I'm working when there's nobody home, Ginny said to drop him round at the antiques shop and he can keep her company 'til someone gets back and collects him."

"Right," said a photographer from the *Pentrillick Gazette*, "I know this is not a joyous occasion but as you're all gathered together can I have a picture please of all the newfound siblings for December's edition."

Irene and Biddy sat down side by side and held hands; behind them, Larry, Harry, Lucky Jim and Norman put down their pints of beer and linked arms.

"Say cheese," said the photographer.

"That'll be an edition to keep," said Lottie.

"Yes, weird, isn't it? They all arrived here looking for something of their past and in doing so have all found each other." Hetty felt quite emotional.

A little later as Hetty returned from the Ladies she cast her eyes across the bar and the couples in particular stood out. Biddy and Geoff, Irene and Jack, Bill and Sandra with arms linked, happy with their new found home. Behind the bar Ashley Rowe whispered something to Alison, his wife and she laughed. Zac, in the games area sat close beside Emma as they watched Jackie play pool with Douglas. Martha and Vicar Sam discreetly held hands. Kitty and her husband Tommy discussed church matters with Debbie and her husband, Gideon. And over by the piano, next door neighbours, Ginny and Alex chatted with Daisy and Eric. Hetty felt a sudden pang of wistfulness and thought of what might have been had she found Mr Right and settled down with him. But then it passed. The feeling of melancholy evaporated. Hetty smiled. She had no regrets nor did she envy any of her friends old and new. In fact at that moment she realised that she was as happy as she had ever been.

Over the roof tops of Pentrillick, a fresh breeze blew up from the sea and swept the grey clouds across the dark sky hiding the stars and the brilliant new moon. Twixt telegraph poles and lamp posts the brightly coloured Christmas lights swayed above fallen leaves as they danced and swirled along the main street towards the Old Bakehouse where Vicki's bunch of mistletoe bobbed and tapped against the bright yellow front door.

On the window ledge sat the robin who frequented the Old Bakehouse garden and he watched as a sprig of mistletoe snapped and broke free; as it fell he plucked it from the air and attempted to fly but the wind was too strong and the mistletoe fell from his beak and blew into the road. The robin gave chase and once more attempted to fly but yet again failed.

On top of a chimney the lone raven flapped his wings and croaked loudly. The robin hopped aside as the big bird swooped down and clasped the mistletoe firmly in its beak; together the two birds then flew over towards the church where the leaves and petals of the freshly laid flowers, piled high on the grave of Geraldine Glover, fluttered and jiggled in the wind.

From the roof of the church porch, the two birds watched as a wreath broke free and tumbled onto the grave of Joseph Percival Williams. Others followed until all wreathes were evenly spread across the two graves like a huge floral blanket. The raven then took flight and dropped the mistletoe onto the bed of flowers where it settled in the middle of Irene's heart shaped holly wreath. And as the two birds flew away to roost, the wind dropped, the grey clouds dispersed and the stars in the dark night sky returned and twinkled brightly around the brilliant new moon.

THE END

Printed in Great Britain
by Amazon